Marriage at

Circle M

DONNA ALWARD

Copyright

the written permission of the publisher, except where permitted by law.

Contents

CHAPTER 1

When Mike Gardner came walking up the path in just *that way*, Grace knew she was in trouble.

And when he stopped at the foot of her stepladder, hooked his thumbs in his jeans pockets, and squinted up at her, she gripped her paintbrush tighter so as not to drop it. Mike was all long, lazy strides and sexy smiles, and despite her best intentions, she'd never been able to remain immune to his charm. Not since she'd hit puberty, anyway.

"Mornin', Grace." The words didn't exactly drawl but were drawn out just enough to give that impression.

Grace straightened her shoulders and did her best to look nonchalant as she swiped another stripe of white paint over the window trim. "Hello, Mike."

Great. Now why in the world did those two words come out all breathless, anyway?

She had to remember that it wasn't all that long go that she'd made a fool of herself where Mike was concerned. It had been years since there had been anything between them. But she'd had a little too much punch, there'd been a little too much giggling and she'd blurted out one very ill-thought-out sentence. She still felt the heat of her embarrassment and every time they met now, she did everything she could to assure him—to assure herself, even—that Mike Gardner was completely resistible. Lord knew he didn't need her fawning over him the way the rest of the female population seemed to. Without thinking, she tucked an errant strand of blond hair behind her ear, leaving it streaked with paint.

"You're up with the birds," he commented, a lazy smile creeping up his cheek as she chanced a look down at him.

"And you knew I would be, or you wouldn't be here so early." She pointedly checked her watch. "It's seven forty-six."

"It is?" His chin flattened ever so slightly. "I'm sorry. I thought it was later."

"You've likely been up and done chores already."

"Yes."

Darn him. She couldn't just stand up on the stepladder like an idiot, carrying on a conversation that was barely holding its own. Besides, she was all too aware that his height, paired with her distance up the ladder, put his line of vision right at her backside. She sighed, put her brush across the top of the paint-smeared can, took a step down...and her dew-slick sneaker slipped on the metal step.

His hands were there to catch her.

"Whoa, there."

She shrugged off his touch. It felt far too strong and too good. "I'm not one of your horses, Mike."

He laughed. "No ma'am. You sure aren't."

It wasn't fair. She'd had a thing for Mike since she was fourteen, but he'd always treated her like a kid sister. An annoying one. For a brief time, when she'd been in high school, they'd been more. But that seemed a lifetime ago. For him to flirt now, weeks after she'd made a complete idiot of herself, it was too much. That one little slip of the lip was the only time she'd ever come close to telling him how she felt, and at the time he'd only laughed at her.

She was older and far wiser now at twenty-seven. There was no room in her life for schoolgirl crushes. She planted her hands on her hips and stared him down. "Look, you obviously didn't come around for idle chit-chat, so tell me what's on your mind so I can get back to work."

Mike had to turn away to hide his smile. She was good and irritated, he could tell. And besides that, she looked wonderful this morning, almost too good. Her honey-blond hair was tucked into some sort of strange clip and little pieces tangled around her ears. Her eyes flashed at him now, icy blue with annoyance. Looking up that stepladder at her slim, tanned legs had almost made him forget why he was here. And steadying her with his arms as she'd slipped had wiped his brain clean of any other thoughts whatsoever. He liked the feel of his hands on her skin.

He stepped back, ignoring her jab, instead turning to survey the small yellow bungalow she called home.

It had seen better days, but Grace had a way of making it welcoming. A caragana hedge flanked the west side of her paved drive —a driveway that was in need of some serious patchwork. He recognized the bleeding-heart shrubs next to some sort of bushes with tiny white flowers. Everything was dressed up by circles of lilies and stalks of purply-blue flowers he remembered from one of his foster homes. The peeling trim on the eaves would soon be gleaming and white like the sections she'd already painted. Somehow, she'd taken a plain, aging bungalow and made it home.

"You're painting."

She kept her eyes front as if refusing to look at him. "Your powers of deduction astound me. What tipped you off?"

He ignored that bit of sarcasm, too. She had to be tired, after all. The drips down the side of her paint can were fresh; she'd obviously been at it a while before he showed up. And he knew for a fact that she'd been up late last night, because her lights had been on when he'd been on his way back from town at nearly one o'clock. He wished she didn't have to work so hard for everything. But he was the last person who could make things better for her. At least for right now he was.

"How do you find time to do everything, Grace? Every time I see you, you're busy at something."

By getting up at five a.m., she thought. Instead she shoved her hands in the pockets of her shorts. "It keeps me out of trouble."

"Then I sure hate to ask what I'm about to."

Mike was serious, she realized, pushing away the urge to use sarcasm as a shield against him. Normally he said nothing at all or what he did say was disarming and funny. But Grace had known him long enough to know when he was troubled. And the tone of his voice right now told her something was definitely going on. When he merely stared at her house longer, she wrinkled her brow and went to him, gently placing a paint-splattered hand on his forearm.

"What's wrong?"

"Connor took Alex to the hospital yesterday afternoon."

Grace's belly twisted at the news. He and Connor were like brothers, so much more than business partners. When Connor had to slaughter his beef herd, he and Mike, long-time friends, had become partners in Circle M Quarter Horses.

"Is it the baby? Are they okay?" Alex looked after the business end now but had a baby due in a few months.

Mike didn't seem to be able to look at her, but she could feel the worry emanating from him. His arm was tense beneath her fingers and his jaw clamped tight. "She went into early labor, so they're keeping her in for a while. Doc says she'll be on bed rest from here on out. That's all I know for now."

"What about Maren?" Grace looked up at his profile. Maren was the couple's toddler, a princess with raven curls and sky-blue eyes like her mother. "Is that why you're here? Do they need someone to watch her for a while?"

"No, no." Mike turned to her then, his lips relaxing just a little. "Connor's grandmother is looking after her. But...I know Alex took over doing the books after she and Connor got married. It's not fair of me to ask, but I was wondering, I mean *we* were wondering, if you'd consider coming back and doing the books for the farm for a while."

If it had been a less serious topic, Grace would have made a quip about that being a regular speech for Mike. Instead, she just nodded. "Of course I will. I don't mind at all."

"It's just that I know you're already busy, and—"

"Mike, it's fine. Alex and Connor are my friends too. I'm happy to help."

His relief was clear. "Thank you, Grace."

It was her own fancy that made his words sound like an endearment. But she knew now that Mike didn't think of her in *that* way anymore. He only looked on her as a friend, she knew that. He'd made it abundantly clear long ago.

She'd already let girlish fantasy rule once in her life and look where that had gotten her. A few troubled years, a whole lot of hurt and then back here in small-town Alberta with a tiny yellow bungalow and a double bed with one pillow.

"You're welcome. I'll try to stop by tomorrow and get things up to speed."

The morning sun grew warmer as they stood on her front lawn, the dew evaporating in the heat. This was just what she needed. To torture herself further by seeing Mike day in and day out at Circle M, a reminder of wanting what she couldn't have. But the truth was, she needed to do some repairs to the house and money was scarce. What she made by doing the odd book work and cleaning jobs didn't leave her with a lot extra at the end of the month. Besides, Mike wouldn't be there all the time now, would he?

"I guess I should be going," he remarked quietly. "I have a few errands and then, well, we're a man short at the ranch. And the building crew comes at nine."

Grace's head swiveled back to him. "Building crew?"

For the first time, Mike really smiled. The effect was devastating, making her heart thump ridiculously in her chest. Darn him for being able to cause such a reaction simply by smiling. His gray-blue eyes lit up as he ran a rough hand through disobedient, coppery hair. "Yeah. We're breaking ground for my new house today."

How did I miss that bit of information? Mike Gardner, with his own business and now a home. Was the eternal drifter really settling down? Wonders never ceased, it seemed.

"Anyway, if you need anything, just call Windover." Mike called the house by its rightful name, even though the now defunct beef ranch was home of Circle M Quarter Horses. "I'm staying there while the house is going up."

Not only at the ranch but living in the house, too. So much for not seeing him, then. And for wanting what she couldn't have. Surely she could stay immune to him for the short term, though, couldn't she?

· · · · · · · · · ·

Grace's hands were devoid of the white paint now, but bits of it still colored her hair. She pulled it back from her face, anchoring the twist blindly with pins at the back of her head. The heat lately had been cloying, and the only way to keep the tender skin of her neck from breaking out was to keep her heavy hair up.

She sighed, turning from the mirror and picking up the light cotton skirt from the foot of the bed.

The reason she kept busy—the real reason she kept taking odd jobs —wasn't really for the money, no matter how much it came in handy.

It was, simply, to keep occupied. To have idle hands meant admitting how empty her life was. How empty it would likely always be. She only had herself to worry about, and that wasn't about to change. And so rather than sit at home, frittering away the time, she worked. Keeping her hands busy helped her forget about the disasters of the past. It gave her less time to sit and think about how everything could go wrong in the blink of an eye. Doing bookwork for the ranch again would fill even more hours.

And she absolutely wasn't putting on a skirt today because she was going out to Circle M, she told herself. The light cotton print was simply cooler than anything else she had in her closet.

As she rolled down the windows of her car, she admitted that extra money wasn't something to scoff at. The vehicle was past its prime and had only been a base model in its newer days. She hadn't had her air conditioning serviced, either, and the interior was sweltering. She pulled out, heading west out of town toward the ranch. The brakes squeaked as she stopped at the intersection to the highway. One of these days she knew the car was going to up and die without any apology.

The drive to Circle M was a pretty one. Now, in late August, there was a hint of gold on the cottonwoods, and the last cut of hay lay in giant green rolls in the fields. Depending on the turn of the road or the elevation, she caught glimpses of the Rocky Mountains, snowless and the unforgiving color of steel. It was, to Grace's mind, an almost perfect time of year. Another few weeks and the temperatures would mellow, the leaves would start to fall, and everything would change from the dry, frantic heat of summer to the mellow, filling warmth of prairie autumn.

Turning north, she smiled at the pastures that had once held Black Angus and now held quarter horses, their hides gleaming in the sun, tails flickering at the flies hovering. Ahead, the main house at Circle M —Windover—stood tall against the azure sky.

It didn't look any different from the outside. But everything else at the ranch had changed.

The barns that had once housed beef cattle now held livestock of the equine variety. Windover Ranch, as it had existed for over a hundred years, was no more, and in its place was Circle M. The disease crisis of a few years back had meant the destruction of Connor's black angus herd, which was almost as surprising as the fact that Mike finally stopped rodeoing and settled down to a full-time, lucrative business.

Seeing Mike on a more regular basis had inspired more than a few dreams on Grace's part. As she pulled up in front of the house, she pressed a hand to her stomach. It had been easier when he hadn't been in town that often. She'd been able to forget about their brief relationship...if it even could have been called a relationship. She'd been seventeen and he'd been twenty-one. For a few weeks they had been more than friends. For a few weeks she'd been blissfully happy.

But when the rodeo season started up again, he went with hardly a word. She'd been okay about it for a long time, or so she thought. The few times their paths had crossed, they'd gone back to being the friends they were before. But now that he was back to stay, seeing him so often brought back longings she thought were dead and buried. She got tongue-tied and bashful. Fiddled with her hair.

No one man should have the power to cause a girl to get so fluttery. She was supposed to be past that by now. She'd left girly behind when she and Steve had signed the divorce papers. When she realized that happily ever after didn't really exist.

The house was quiet when she knocked, so she wandered around to the side of the house in case someone was outside.

She was in luck. Johanna, Connor's grandmother, was kneeling at a small flower garden with the curly-topped Maren babbling happily at her side.

"Good morning, Mrs. Madsen."

Johanna's head turned, a smile lighting up her face. "Grace, dear. It's so good to see you." Rising, she brushed off the knees of her slacks and held out a hand to the toddling baby beside her. "Maren, you remember Grace, don't you?"

Maren suddenly fell silent and plopped a thumb into her mouth, and Grace laughed.

"She probably doesn't remember me. I haven't been around much."

"That's about to change, isn't it?"

Grace nodded at Johanna, the two exchanging a solemn look. "I thought I'd stop in today and get up to speed."

"Connor and Mike are both out, but you're no stranger to the setup. I know they're both happy you're here."

"How is Alex, then?"

"Being monitored." Johanna picked up the baby and climbed the steps to the deck. "So far she's doing okay, but at thirty-two weeks..."

"They want to buy her—and the baby—some more time." Grace followed Johanna inside, standing back as Maren was placed in her highchair.

"Exactly. The doctor said that even another couple of weeks can make a big difference with the baby's lungs. Of course, Connor's worried sick."

Johanna put a sippy cup in front of Maren. "Connor's spending almost all his time at the hospital, and Mike isn't meant for bookwork, so I'm glad you're here to help."

"I'd do anything for...to help," she finished, coloring at her almost mistake. Even if she knew she'd do anything for Mike, she didn't need the rest of the world to know it. Thankfully Johanna seemed oblivious as she busied herself making iced tea.

The front door slammed, and Grace jumped. When Mike strode into the kitchen, she took a step back, her gaze drawn undeniably towards his.

God, he looked fabulous. All coiled strength in his faded jeans and corded muscles beneath a blue T-shirt. His hat, the cream-colored Stetson he never worked without, was on his head, but when he saw her standing there he automatically reached up to remove it.

It was August. His hair clung to his scalp in dark curls and Grace watched as one solitary bead of sweat trickled from one temple down his jaw.

Maren smacked her cup on the tray of her chair while Johanna watched, clearly intrigued with the silent interplay between the couple.

"Grace."

"Mike." His name sounded strangled to her as it came out of her mouth. And she knew she was glad she'd chosen a skirt and pretty blouse after all.

"I, uh, just came to get something to drink."

"I think Johanna's making some iced tea."

Still their gazes clung, and she remembered the feel of his hands on her arms yesterday morning. He swallowed, his Adam's apple bobbing. Goodness, they were staring at each other like idiots.

He broke away first. "Iced tea sounds perfect, but you're not here to look after me, Mrs. Madsen."

Johanna poured three glasses without batting an eye. "I'd like to know where all this Mrs. Madsen nonsense came from all of a sudden. I've known both of you so long I used to wipe your runny noses, so call me Johanna or Gram like everyone else."

Mike's lips quivered as he struggled not to smile. The Madsen's were as close to family as he had, not counting his cousin Maggie.

Johanna took one look at Maren and plucked the girl up from her chair. "I'll just go change the baby," she suggested blandly. "Grace, I'm sure you remember your way to the office."

"Of course I do. I'll sort things out, not to worry."

"I'm sure you Mike will help you. Won't you, Mike?"

His lips pursed together, and he let his eyes twinkle at the older woman. "Indeed I will...Gram."

Her rusty laugh disappeared with the baby, and he was left with Grace.

She looked beautiful today. As usual. But he thought he saw hints of purple beneath her eyes. Lord only knew what work she'd taken on now. She was always working. And now he'd helped her exhaustion along by asking for a favor. He should have found another way.

But another way would have meant that he wouldn't have excuse to see her. And after she'd let the cat out of the bag, so to speak, at the Riley's anniversary party, he thought about seeing her more and more. He'd been shocked to say the least, but not unpleasantly. Knowing Grace still felt some attraction for him seemed to legitimize his own for her. He'd let her get away once before, and had always been sorry. But knowing she still thought of him in *that* way changed everything. Heck, not that he'd admit it to her, but he'd made the excuse for a mid-morning drink just because he'd seen her car pull into the yard.

Her hair was sneaking out of the twist, curling around her temples in damp tendrils. The warmth of the morning gave a glow to her skin. To him, she was a picture of femininity, of innocence, purity. Certainly too fine of a woman for a man like him to tangle with.

"You're looking tired. I hope this extra won't put unnecessary strain on you."

That was it? Grace tried to keep her lips from falling open but failed. All those long stares and all he came up with was "you're looking tired"? Her elation at seeing him flew out the window.

"Your compliments make a girl all warm and fuzzy."

He at least had the decency to look chagrined. "I didn't mean to say you looked bad."

"Even better. You know, I can't imagine what the women around here see in you."

It was out before she could think better of it, and she instantly flushed. They both knew it was a lie. He knew very well that she *was* one of those women. She'd said it herself as they'd danced. She covered the slip with more offensive.

"But I can assure you I can handle a little *unnecessary strain*, as you put it. I'm not made of china, Michael." She used his full name and watched his lip curl a little. She knew how much he hated being called Michael.

Mike had put his hat back on, the brim shading his eyes and making him look even larger than his six-foot-two frame.

"Is there anything I can do to help you, then?"

Grace looked up and saw his eyes were earnest even though his tone was cold, and she nearly backed down. She acknowledged the attraction, but that was where it stopped. Mike didn't feel anything for her, that much was clear. Men who were interested told you how nice you looked, gave you compliments instead of remarking on the presence of bags beneath your eyes or asking you to balance the books. She'd done the longing gaze thing for far too many years, and it had gotten her nowhere. It hadn't been enough before. And it wouldn't get her anywhere in the future, either. Men didn't want women like her, not once they realized that she was more than the quiet, girl-next-door that they thought she was.

"Yes, Mike, there is something you can do for me. You can get out of the way and let me do my job."

CHAPTER 2

Grace shut the checkbook and sighed. Alex had done a good job with the books, but she *was* behind by a month or two. Not much wonder, Grace thought, taking a brain break. She leaned back in the desk chair and took a sip of her soda. Alex was pregnant, chasing after a toddler, and summer was the busiest time on a farm. Now it was up to Grace to straighten things out and keep things up to date. Even if Alex did get home soon, she was under orders for bed rest, and then after the baby came, she'd be too exhausted to worry about payables and receivables. Grace wasn't sure if being close to Mike so often was going to be a blessing or a curse.

But luckily for Alex, Grace was all too happy to fill in. She loved accounting. It was gratifying to see all those numbers line up just right and have things balance out at the end of the day. It was neat and orderly, and every time she finished running a report or balancing an account, she got this great sense of accomplishment. With so much of her life feeling arbitrary and out of sync, balancing those columns was like *something* in her life was where it was supposed to be.

The downside was that in order to put food on the table, she had to do other jobs just to make ends meet. It was a small town, and without her CPA, she didn't make enough to pay the bills with the few accounting jobs she had. She hired herself out as a cleaning lady as well. It supplemented her income and, to be honest, kept her from being too lonely. Yesterday she'd spent the entire day cleaning for Mrs.

Darrin. When the cleaning was finished, she'd planned to go back home and finish painting the trim on her house. But Mrs. Darrin was feeling poorly and had asked Grace to tend to her garden as well, so Grace stayed and cut the grass and weeded the feeble flower bed in front of the house. After that, she'd stayed for tea. She appreciated the social contact almost as much as the paycheck. But because she'd put in a longer day, she'd been up since five this morning, finishing up the painting so she could spend the day at Windover.

"How's it going?"

She swiveled hard in her chair, her hand swinging out so that some of the liquid splashed out of the soda can and landed on her white capris. She scowled up at Mike, her heart pounding from the sight of him standing in the doorway. He was so tall in his boots that it seemed that his head almost grazed the top of the door frame.

"God, Mike, how on earth do you manage to sneak up on someone like that?"

"I made enough noise to wake the dead. You were in the zone."

Zoned out, more like it, but she wouldn't admit that.

And how disgusting was it that even when he wandered into the study, smelling of perspiration and horses, her pulse quickened? Her eyes lit on a rivulet of sweat beaded at the hollow of his throat. There was something so elementally attractive about a hardworking man. Something that didn't come with expensive toiletries and business suits. It was that little bit of dirt, the little bit of scruff, and the dedication and muscle it took to do what he did. When she didn't say anything back to him, he raised one eyebrow in question.

"You...you don't have your hat on," she stammered, immediately feeling stupid at such an inane comment.

His other eyebrow lifted. "It's around here somewhere."

Oh, this was crazy. Every time he was out of the way she swore she wouldn't be so affected the next time they met. Promised herself she'd forget about the past. Then the moment she saw him she became a babbling idiot. She turned away from him deliberately, picking up her red pen and twisting it in her fingers.

"I still have work to do, so unless there's something you needed..."

Even without his customary hat, he towered above her until he knelt by her chair. His knees cracked as he squatted, balancing on the heels of his boots. He put a hand on the arm of her chair and swung it a little, so she was turned toward him.

"I came to ask another favor. I'd ask Johanna, but—"

"But a woman her age...chasing after a nearly two-year-old is taking its toll on her. I know. What's up?"

He lifted his gray eyes to her. It was like magnets of opposite poles, when she met his eyes with her own, pulling them together. Like nearly ten years hadn't elapsed and they were back in Lloyd Andersen's meadow on a cool Sunday morning. She was unable to turn away, instead drawn into the earnest depths.

"Alex is coming home tonight, and I wondered, that is...I know she's supposed to be on bed rest and all, but..."

His words drew her out of her reverie. "You want to do something nice?"

"Yeah." He smiled a little sheepishly and her heart warmed. It was one of the things she liked about him. He came across as all male and tough, then at the most unexpected times showed a thoughtful side.

"And you want me to help."

"It's not like I know much about this kind of thing. And Connor's with Alex and not here to see to it."

"I can make a special dinner," she replied. "Dress Maren up in something pretty, make it a low-key welcome home with just the family."

"Thank you, Grace. That's perfect."

She had a dirty house of her own, but it didn't matter very much right now. She sighed. It wasn't like anyone was going to see it besides herself. Spending the evening with the Madsen's was just what the doctor ordered.

Mike heard the sigh and misinterpreted it. "I'm sorry, I probably shouldn't have asked." He straightened his knees, looming above her once more. "You're already busy and tired. I can just order something in."

"No, it's not that, I'm happy to…"

His mood changed so quickly her head spun. His lips thinned and his jaw hardened at her words. He almost seemed like he was angry at her, and she didn't have an idea why.

"You always are, Grace. *Happy to.* Every time someone asks for a favor, there you are. You're working yourself to death, and for what? You're clearly exhausted. Ordering in might be better anyway, and that way you get a break. Get some rest. I should have thought of it sooner."

Here he was again, telling her how tired she looked. Her temper fired. What did Mike know about anything? And who was he to tell her what to do? He'd never asked for her input before, not even when they'd been dating. He'd just been…gone. That certainly hadn't earned him the right to start dictating things now. "You know what, Mike? I'm a big girl. I think I know my own limits."

"I don't think you do." His voice was sharp, and her eyebrows lifted at the tone. "You'd work yourself into the ground if I let you. Don't worry about dinner. Forget I mentioned it."

"You know, you're really starting to piss me off," she answered, the words low. It might have sounded threatening to someone other than Mike, but there wasn't much that got under his skin, and it was another thing about him that was making her mad right at that moment. "If you *let* me? I don't recall requiring your permission,

Mike Gardner. If I didn't have time to do it, I'd say so. When has it ever been a hardship spending time with Connor and Alex? It just so happens my evening is free, so there."

Great. Now, in her anger, she'd made it sound like she had no social life whatsoever.

"And you could spend it sleeping, from the looks of it," he continued, undeterred by her sharp tone. "I see how hard you work, Grace. You clean half the town and do books for the other half. You're on just about everyone's 'fill-in' list and if there's something going on, you're in the thick of it! One of these days you're going to make yourself sick!"

She stood from her chair, tears of absolute anger threatening. "Who in the world do you think you are, to criticize me?" She was gratified when he took a step back. "Who died and made you my sole protector and guardian?"

"Well, someone clearly has to, if you're not going to look after yourself!" His voice thundered through the room as they argued.

"I'm a grown woman, in case you hadn't noticed!"

"Oh, I noticed all right!" He blurted it out, then everything fell silent.

He noticed, her heart rejoiced. *Stop it, you ninny,* she chided herself on the back of the thought. She was supposed to be infuriated with him right now. She *was* angry. She was in no mood to be played with. Not by Mike, not by anyone.

She cleared her throat, letting her hands drop to her sides. "Good, then. I'm glad we straightened that out. Now get out of my way so I can get started. If I'm making dinner, I need to finish this up." She sent him a withering look. "*Without* your interference."

Mike turned on a heel. Get out of her way? No problem! Not when she attacked him like that. She could just forget about him showing any concern for her welfare again!

He stalked out of the house, heading towards the east section where the concrete foundation for his house was being poured. Grace didn't understand anything.

He'd always thought of her as a kid sister. When he'd finally settled here in eighth grade, she'd been in fourth. When he'd graduated high school, she'd just finished middle school and hadn't even really sprouted breasts yet.

Then she had grown up, and he'd taken notice. She'd been a picture of innocent beauty, and for a while he'd let himself care about her. He'd let her care about him. For a brief time, he'd let his heart dictate his actions instead of his head. He'd held her, kissed her. Cherished her like she deserved. But he'd fallen too fast, and he knew once she saw him for who he really was, she'd cut and run. So he'd made sure he'd done the running first. As soon as the rodeo season started up that year, he'd hit the road and hadn't looked back.

When she'd moved back after her divorce he'd been in town for a few weeks and was floored the first time he saw her. He kicked at the dry path with a leather toe, sending up a puff of dust. The years had made full the promise of the woman he'd thought she'd become. She was more than beautiful. She was exactly what a woman should be. Her beauty was natural, pure. It shone out from her, lit up by her generous heart and kind manner. The fact that her husband had seen fit to break her heart...he'd stewed about that one for a good long time, even partially blamed himself. It was a good thing the jerk didn't live close by. Mike didn't tend to let people get away with treating his friends like dirt beneath their shoes.

Because she was his friend, first and foremost, and he was torn between the girl she'd been and the woman she'd become. Stupid thing was, he had this uncanny urge to protect them both.

He wandered through the jobsite, joking with the men, grabbing a shovel and helping out. Still, she remained on his mind. Earlier in the summer, at the anniversary party for the Riley's, Grace had indulged in a few too many vodka coolers and he'd laughingly danced with her. Old friends. Only she'd smiled up at him widely and said, "Mike, you're so pretty."

He'd made a joke of it, but she'd been undaunted. "I bet you're good in the sack, too. We've been ssspeculating." She swept an arm to encompass a group of young women, all giggling behind their hands and watching Mike and Grace dance. "All that...mmmmm," she'd finished, her eyelids drifting closed as she swayed her hips to the music.

He'd been shocked, to put it mildly, and more than a little embarrassed. Grace had come on to him and he hadn't had a clue how to answer. He'd thought she'd put their fling in the past, especially when she'd moved to Edmonton and married. Heck, he'd only been back in town permanently since spring, setting up business with Connor. As they moved to the music, her curves felt soft and sexy in his arms and he'd asked plainly, "You think about that?"

She'd suddenly seemed to realize what she'd said, because her posture straightened and she'd colored to the hue of fireweed. "Shut up," she'd snapped, trying to cover. "Don't let it go to your head."

Her quick change of tone had relaxed him, giving him the upper hand again and he'd managed to tease her about it.

But the problem was, it *had* gone to his head. He'd done nothing but think of it since. Wondering how they'd be together. Wanting to kiss her, wondering if it would be the same as he remembered. Wanting to hold her—all night long. In his mind he could imagine what being with Grace would be like.

But Grace deserved more than an ex-saddle bronc rider with a spotted past, and he knew it. And somehow, he was going to show her that he was more than that. He just needed more time.

· · • • · • • • · ·

Mike halted before the screen door, taking a deep breath. He'd been too hard on Grace. He hated seeing her working so hard, but somehow all his well-intentioned concern had come out wrong and she'd gotten angry with him. Hopefully she wasn't still, but just in case, he'd cut across the field and come home along the ditch after leaving the building site.

He resisted the strange urge to knock. Instead, he swung the door open with an arthritic creak and stepped inside.

He left his boots on the mat and made his way to the kitchen. He stopped in the doorway, watching Grace as she moved about the room.

Her pants and blouse were protected by a flowered cobbler apron that she'd borrowed, presumably from Johanna. As she carried plates to the table, the scent of frying chicken filled the air.

"Your table's missing something."

Her head snapped up. "When did you come in?"

A flippant comment about her not hearing him enter sat on his tongue, but he kept it in. He didn't want to pick another fight by bugging her about it. "Just a minute ago. Supper smells great."

She resumed setting the table. "It's just chicken and salads. Something we can eat whenever they arrive. I dressed Maren and Johanna took her to the hospital. They're all coming back together."

"I thought you could use some decoration." He stepped inside the room, holding out his hand.

"Flowers. You picked flowers?" Her fingers put down the cutlery as she stared at him.

"I thought they might make things a little more special." He handed them to her, a mass of daisies and greenery he couldn't name but knew by sight. He hadn't picked weeds for a woman since he was in primary school, and he'd tried to impress one of his foster moms.

Grace took the blooms from his hand, and he suddenly realized that he hadn't exactly given them to *her*. He'd made it sound like they were for a centerpiece, that was all.

"I also thought they might soften you up for my apology."

Her hands stilled over the vase she'd taken from the top of a pine buffet in the corner. "Apology?"

"I'm sorry we fought earlier." He couldn't bring himself to say he was sorry for everything. He found he wasn't sorry for being concerned about her welfare. But he was sorry for upsetting her.

She turned to look at him, the vase of flowers in her hands. "I am, too."

Their gazes met across the room. Lord, she had a way of looking at a man that made him want to do all sorts of things for her. Her lips were open just a hint, ripe for kissing, and her eyes were soft and wide. For a fleeting moment he wondered what she'd do if he simply closed the distance between them and kissed her like he'd wanted to for weeks. But the timing was wrong, and the moment passed. Grace looked away.

"I was just worried, that's all. I've known you a long time, Grace. I just want you to look after yourself."

She put the flowers in the middle of the table and stood back. "Thanks for your concern, Mike, but it's not necessary. I've been looking after myself for a while now." She moved back to the stove, taking the lid off the electric frying pan and capably turning the chicken with a set of tongs.

Of course she had, he acknowledged silently. She'd been back in town for what, five or six years? Living on her own all that time. Without him. But that didn't stop the protective streak that seemed to rear its head every time she was around.

The screen door opened, and voices filtered through the hall to the kitchen. "I think they've arrived," Grace remarked, grabbing a platter.

"Timing's good too. Chicken's done."

When Alex and Connor entered, Maren on Connor's arm, Mike forced a smile. "Welcome home."

Alex's eyes filled with tears. "Oh, you guys, you shouldn't have." She walked carefully, like she was afraid of breaking something. She looked over her shoulder at Johanna, then to the stove and Grace who was standing with the platter of chicken in her hands.

"You did this?"

"It was Mike's idea. Be thankful I did the cooking and not him."

Everyone laughed, including Mike who agreed. "I'll make the coffee. Everything else I'll trust to Grace."

"Wise move," Grace countered, but he was gratified to see her treat him to a genuine smile.

Alex's smile widened and she leaned up to give Mike a quick hug. "You softie," she whispered in his ear.

"Be quiet, that's a secret," he whispered back. Straightening, he chided her. "No work. We're going to look after everything so you can just look after that bundle in there." He pointed at her belly.

"That's what I've been telling her," Connor said, putting Maren in her highchair and handing her a cracker. "Nothing's more important than looking after our baby."

Mike looked at Grace. Her face carried a strange expression as she looked at Alex. He'd almost swear she looked...wounded, he supposed. Her eyes were luminous, wide with hurt. He'd never quite seen that look before and didn't know what to make of it. There was concern, he was sure, but there was something else. A deep, lingering sadness. But why would seeing Alex make her sad?

She caught him watching her and pasted on a smile, the expression disappearing as if it had never been. "Put the chicken on, will you Mike? I'll get the rest of the food out of the fridge."

They all sat down to a celebratory dinner, but Mike couldn't forget that haunted look on Grace's face.

· · · · ·· · · · ·

Connor and Alex were putting Maren to bed; Johanna was cleaning up the kitchen. Grace had tried to help, but Johanna had shooed her away, saying the cooks didn't need to wash dishes. Grace knew she should just get in her car and go home, but instead she wandered out to the garden in the twilight, smelling the fragrant sweet peas that climbed the white lattice pergola.

The moon started its ascent. Frogs chirped from the pond down behind the barn. Grace sighed. If she went home now, she'd end up feeling sorry for herself and spending the evening with a bowl of ice cream and a box of tissues. Despite the worry of the present, the Madsens were a happy family. Strong and bonded. She'd thought she'd have that, once, but now knew it would never happen. Most times she was okay with it. But times like this... Oh, times like this it hit her hard, made her mourn what she'd lost and what she'd never have.

She'd never have her own family.

"Beautiful night, isn't it?"

Mike's voice interrupted the quiet sounds of dusk and Grace swallowed the ball of emotion that had gathered in her throat. "Sure is."

"You going to tell me what's making you so blue?"

He was standing a little behind her and she kept her back to him. If she looked at him she wasn't sure she wouldn't lose it, and what an awkward mess that would be.

"I'm fine. Just enjoying the evening."

"Grace Lundquist, you're a bad liar."

She sighed, willing him to stay behind her. Her eyes closed. "Just leave it be, Mike."

He was quiet for a moment and Grace wondered if he'd gone. Then his voice came back, low and rumbly.

"I can't."

Oh, why did he have to be so concerned and caring all of a sudden? Mike didn't think of her in any way besides a friend, and even if he did, it wouldn't make sense to pursue anything, no matter how long she'd crushed on him. He didn't stay anywhere for long, or with anyone. In all the years she'd known him, he'd only had brief, fun relationships. Nothing serious. And Grace didn't do brief and fun.

She had, once. And she'd thought Mike had really cared about her. She supposed in his own way, he had. But not enough. He hadn't even broken up with her. He'd just been *gone*.

She cared about him, yes. She admitted that much to herself. But she couldn't let herself get too close. She didn't trust him not to leave her again, and she wasn't into making the same mistake twice.

No, they'd get along much better if they stuck to friends only.

His hand rested on her shoulder, and she leaned into the reassuring contact. "I'm okay. I promise."

"You didn't look fine at dinner. You looked like your whole world was crashing in around you."

Grace forced a smile and finally turned to meet his gaze. His eyes were dark with concern as his hand slid from her shoulder down to grip her fingers.

She pulled her hand away, attempting a laugh. "When did you get so dramatic, Mike? Worlds crashing around. As if."

"If you weren't upset, then what are you doing out here in the dark?"

"I didn't want to intrude. I should just head home."

A horse whickered softly in the moonshine. Mike turned his head towards the sound, smiling a little. "You shouldn't worry about intruding. I'm living here. You can't get much more in the way than that."

"It's only temporary."

"Yes, it is. I'm looking forward to having my own place."

Grace studied him, glad that the topic of conversation had been diverted away from her. He'd spent so many years without roots. Other than Maggie, his cousin-turned-foster parent, he'd never had a home. It just hadn't been his way. A home had always seemed to represent a commitment he didn't want to make.

"It seems funny, thinking of you with your own house, tied to a business. You've never been that type of guy."

His gray eyes penetrated hers. "I wasn't, not for a long time. Things change."

"What things?" She tilted her head curiously.

"It didn't make sense to roam around without a purpose, looking for something yet not knowing what *it* was. I found myself wanting to settle, find a place for me. Build a business. Make a home, maybe even have a family."

And just like that, her world dropped out from under her. It was like her bones had suddenly turned to jelly and everything got too heavy to move. He watched her quietly, his strong body between her and the house.

She had to escape.

Mike and a house and a family. Words she never thought she'd ever hear out of his lips.

Why had it taken him so long to figure it out? If only he hadn't taken a decade, things might have been different after all. A whole can of "what if's" was opened, the contents spilled out.

After the long, emotional day she'd had, it was too much. Her eyes burned with tears she tried desperately to hold inside, and her mouth twisted. She chewed on her lip to keep it from quivering.

"I've gotta go," she choked out, pushing past him and making a run for her car. She wrenched open the door and got in, turned the key to the ignition.

Just her luck. The one thing Mike was looking for now was the very thing she'd never be able to give him.

CHAPTER 3

Grace dragged herself out of bed. With a stroke of impeccable timing, she'd caught an early fall cold and it had completely knocked her out. Her head felt like a giant boulder sitting atop her neck, which might have been all right if only she could have breathed. But no, her nose was plugged, her throat was sore, and the only thing she wanted was to stay in bed and hide under the covers. Which was a crying shame, because outside everything was gilded and warm. The leaves were changing, her asters were blooming, and bees hummed lazily in the mellow autumn sunshine.

With the teakettle on, she suddenly realized that tomorrow was payday at Circle M. Alex was confined to bed; it was up to her to make sure the checks got written. She sat at the table, resting her plugged head on her hands. No way was she heading out to the ranch. The last thing Alex—or Maren—needed was for her to pass on her cold. Ugh. This would be so much easier if the ranch had set up direct deposit.

Maybe someone from Circle M could drop off the paperwork and checkbook, she thought, getting up to pour the boiling water in her mug. Inspired, she picked up the phone and made the necessary call. After hanging up, she took the bag from her cup and added a squirt of lemon juice and a teaspoon of honey. Perhaps after her cup of tea she'd run a hot bath and try to steam away the congestion. And then maybe, just maybe, she'd feel human again.

．．．．．．．．．．．

Mike pulled into the drive, grabbed the files from the passenger seat, and hopped out of the truck. He skirted around the hood, heading for the back door. Grace rarely used the front; it was a porch filled with natural light and plants and where he knew she liked to sit with a book, letting the breeze blow through the windows. He'd just drop off the ledger and checkbook, make sure she was okay, and be on his way. Lord knew there was no shortage of work at Circle M lately. At least Connor was back, now that Alex was out of hospital.

It seemed to take Grace a long time to answer his knock, and when she did it took all he had not to gape.

She was dressed in snug jeans and a silky blue top that made his mouth water. He swallowed. The soft fabric dipped to a "v" in the front, triangling the shape of her breasts, then flowing in folds to her waist. The sleeves clung to her upper arms, draping away gracefully past her elbows. It was a combination of innocent and sexy and for a brief moment he envisioned himself sliding his fingers over her soft shoulders while he kissed the daylights out of her.

The towel wrapped turban-style around her head might have made that difficult, however.

"I'm interrupting."

"It's okay." The words came out "it-th ok." The steamy bath hadn't relieved all of her congestion. She sniffled, tried again. "Come on in."

Mike followed her in, still holding the materials she'd need to do payroll, his customary hat still shielding his eyes.

"Thank you, Mike, for delivering the books."

"Your cold sounds bad." When Johanna had told him that Grace was sick, his first thought hadn't been about working with the horses or helping with the construction of his house. Instead he'd volunteered to be a delivery boy. He'd thought he could make sure she was all right after her outburst the other night. He wanted to take care of her. There was something about Grace that inspired that urge to protect, even though he knew she deserved better.

"I tried tea and honey and I took a decongestant, but it hasn't kicked in yet," she explained, leaning back against the kitchen counter.

"Yes, well, you can drop off the checks when they're done then. Payday is tomorrow, but the guys'll understand if you're a little late. You deserve a day in bed."

Grace looked up into Mike's eyes and he noticed how flushed and pretty she looked. The thought of her in bed didn't help his current mental state either.

"I'll have them there on time, you know that."

"It's okay. You need to rest," he insisted.

"Someone make you a doctor all of a sudden?" She drew away from the counter, crossing her arms in front of her.

His chin drew back at the sharp edge of her tone. "You're sick. It happens to everyone."

"Exactly. And the world doesn't stop just because someone has the sniffles. I said I'd have them done and I will. Besides, I have other work besides Circle M. I don't want to get behind."

"Work, work. That's all you ever do." The words burst out of his mouth before he could stop them. Why was she being so stubborn? All he was trying to do was cut her some slack, and she wouldn't have any of it.

Grace put her hands on her hips as the towel slipped sideways on her head. *Here we go again,* she thought. Yes, she worked a lot, but it wasn't like she had a family at home to look after. It was just her, and more than that, it was her time to do with what she wished. She'd bought this house all on her own after the divorce, and without a regular nine-to-five job, sometimes making the mortgage payment was difficult. Not to mention repairs and the fact that she tried to make it look like a home...and all that cost money. Instead she had to deal with Mike today, coming in and bossing her around. There was four years difference in their ages, but that gap had all but disappeared since the first time he'd kissed her. So why he felt it was his right to treat her like the girl who used to tag along after him, she had no idea.

"Yes, I work a lot. In case you haven't noticed, I don't have an overflowing social calendar and like the rest of the world I have bills to pay."

She spun away, angry with herself for letting Mike provoke her. The towel slipped all the way off and she caught it, while strands of dark blond hair straggled down her back. With her free hand she pushed them back out of her face.

He studied her for a long moment before speaking.

"You having money troubles, Grace?" He said it quietly. Not criticizing. The way Mike, her old friend would have. His obvious caring was comforting in a way.

But seeing Mike lately was only making her more confused. She cared about him, always had. Yet he'd broken a bit of that trust, and she couldn't forget it. At the same time, knowing he was there, in her corner, made her feel like she could rely on him. And it was that fact that had kept their friendship alive through the intervening years.

"No, I'm not," she sighed. "But my cup doesn't runneth over, either."

"Let me help."

She looked up into his eyes, faltering for a moment at the genuine concern she saw there. But no, it wasn't Mike's problem, and she'd learned long ago that she could only depend on herself. She squared her shoulders.

"Thanks, but I'm fine. I *like* working, Mike."

"Aren't I allowed to be concerned about you?"

She sniffled once more and tucked her untidy hair behind her ears. "I'm not twelve any more Mike, and you don't need to keep the playground bullies in line." She swallowed, struggling to keep her voice cool and even.

He laughed, lightening the mood a little. "Seems to me there was a time that *you* kept the bullies in line for *me*."

She flushed, wishing he'd just forget about that. Even as a child, she'd stood up for him when others didn't. She knew now how silly it must have looked, a little squirt of a thing taking up for a boy much older than she'd been.

"Thanks for your concern, but I'm fine. You must have work to do today. I'll bring the checks over when they're done."

She didn't wait for him to leave but took the books from the table and went into the living room. When the back screen clicked quietly, she let out a long breath.

· · • • • • • • · ·

Mike gave Thunder's chestnut hide a final affectionate slap and left the stall, shutting the half-door behind him. He'd bought Thunder and Lightning together as colts, the first horses he'd owned. They'd been named by the previous owner's young son, and while Mike thought of changing their names to something less clichéd, one look at the boy's crestfallen face had sealed the deal. When he'd loaded them into the trailer, he'd promised that he'd keep the names that the youngster had given them. And he'd kept that promise.

Lightning was out in the corral. Thunder was inside today, waiting for the farrier. The last thing Mike needed now was a lame animal.

Over the years his path had crossed with Grace's, and during those times he'd always looked out for her, whether she knew it or not. He'd been off on the circuit when she'd met her husband, and when he'd come back, she was already gone...married at nineteen and living in

Edmonton. He couldn't change that. He had been the one to leave, after all.

Over the years he'd passed through town occasionally and it struck him that she'd been so sad when she'd moved into the tiny bungalow all alone. He saw glimpses of that sadness still. It made him want to bundle her in his arms and make it better. He wanted Grace for himself. In every way, no matter how much she deserved better. For a long time, he'd despaired of it ever happening, thinking he'd squandered his chance. But now...now he was back for good, and he knew if he bided his time, did things right, there was hope.

He strode down the length of the barn, his boots echoing on the concrete floor. Reaching the door, he saw her car come creeping up the drive. She was true to her word no matter how sick she was. The paychecks would be handed out on time. His face darkened with a scowl.

He should walk away, let her deliver her things to the office and leave again. Instead, he left the barn door open and strode toward the house.

· · · · · · · · · · ·

This time Grace heard him open the front door. She'd been listening for it, to be honest, and had chosen to stay in the kitchen rather than the intimate, closed space of the study. She didn't plan to stay long; she didn't want to spread her germs to either Alex or Maren. Mike had been such a hardheaded idiot at the house earlier. She had to keep her cool. The last thing she wanted was yet another spat with him. It seemed to be all they did lately, and she didn't quite understand why.

She made her hands busy, stuffing checks in envelopes and writing names on the front. She didn't look up from her work but knew when he was at the threshold. The air simply changed.

"Hello Mike. Got your checks done."

He stepped in. "That's great. I'm glad you could fit it into your busy schedule."

When she looked up, it was work to keep her mouth from dropping open. Mike looked...formidable, standing squarely in the doorway, his hat still on his head and his jaw so tensed it almost made a right angle.

She took a deep breath, willing herself to stay calm. Funny how by just standing there, he could provoke her. His whole manner told her he was angry about something, although she didn't have a blessed idea what it was this time. Still, she attempted a light smile as she responded.

"I took some meds and had a nap." The words were slightly thick; the congestion hadn't quite cleared, although she was feeling much better. The tip of her nose wasn't even showing that much redness anymore. "It was no trouble getting them drawn up."

She turned her attention back to the envelopes. "I wanted to get them here. I have a couple of jobs lined up for tomorrow."

"While you're sick?"

"I'm much better, thank you, and for your information my plan was to go home, make some soup, and watch a movie with a blanket before falling blissfully into sleep and waking up completely cured." She didn't even attempt to keep the sarcasm out of her tone.

Mike waited several seconds before speaking again.

"It didn't occur to you to maybe rest for a few days? Do you have a hard time telling people the word no?" he bit out.

She goggled at his sharp tone. So much for keeping her cool and not letting him get to her. "As a matter of fact, I don't. How's this? Do I want to discuss this with you again? No!" She spun away, fiddling with papers on the table without really seeing.

Why, oh why, was everything an argument with Mike lately? He'd always had this protective streak when it came to people he cared about. People like herself, like Connor. But lately, it was different. He acted almost like he was entitled to have a say in how she lived her life, and he absolutely did not.

"You couldn't have heard me this morning." She tried to muster her iciest tone but failed when her plugged nose interfered. "I'm not discussing my schedule or health with you."

"Well, that's just fine." Mike swept an arm wide. "That's just great, Grace!"

The checks were forgotten behind her as she squared off. "You know, Mike, I'm not fond of this proprietary attitude you seem to have lately. What gives you the right to dictate to me how I live my life?"

"The right?" He took two steps forward until she had to tilt her chin to meet his gaze. "The fact that you obviously need someone to, instead of letting you make bad decisions!" His voice thundered throughout the room.

"Keep your voice down," she warned. "There are other people in this house who are probably trying to rest."

He shoved his hands into his pockets but didn't move.

"This is my life, Mike," she whispered harshly. "My decisions to make. My mistakes. Nobody—and that definitely includes you—is going to tell me what I can or can't do. Frankly, going to work when one has a cold can hardly be called a bad decision."

"I hate it that you look out for everyone else but yourself. Someday, Grace, that's going to catch up with you, and then where will you be?"

With a sigh, he dropped his shoulders from their offensive stance.

Surprise had her rooted to the spot when he lifted his hand and his fingers grazed the soft skin of her cheek.

"I just want to look out for you."

The resistance drained from her body as her eyes fluttered closed against his touch, so suddenly tender and gentle. "I can look after myself."

"Maybe." He lifted his other hand so that now both his thumbs gently rubbed the crests of her cheekbones.

Her breath caught in her throat as she opened her eyes to find Mike's staring down at her. Staring through her, right into her core, it seemed, his gray eyes shadowed by the brim of his hat.

"Why does it matter to you?"

"It matters." His gaze dipped to her lips and clung there. "You matter."

She swallowed. She mattered? To Mike? And he wasn't looking at her now like he usually did. For the most part it was like they had never been more, like it was a blip on the road to where they were now. But now...friends didn't stare at lips the way he was looking at hers, or let their fingers caress cheeks.

Still cupping her jaws, he leaned in, his mouth only a breath away as he whispered, "I just can't let you get hurt, Grace..."

She reached up, circled his wrists with her hands, and pulled them away from her face. She stepped back, putting distance between them. Longing still curled through her, a yearning that was almost too strong. She could feel his arms around her even though it had never happened. And it would be wrong, she realized.

"You can't let me?" Her words were soft in the confused silence. She chanced a look at Mike. He was rooted to the spot, his brows pulled together. He didn't understand. It was even more reason for her to pull away.

"You don't get it, Mike. You say *you* can't let me get hurt. And I can't let you make decisions for me." *Not again,* she almost added.

"Even when you make mistakes?"

"Then they'll be my mistakes, not yours. Thank you for your concern, but it's unwarranted."

"You almost kissed me a moment ago."

Her tummy flopped over. Yes, she had. And her body still hummed, yearning to know if kissing Mike would be the same. Or different. Or better. She'd been *that* close.

"I think you almost kissed me." She tried to joke but it fell flat.

"Don't do that. Don't change the subject. There's more going on here than you'll admit."

Memory hummed between them, drawing out the silence. What if things were changing between them? What then? Would he back off, leave her when it suited him? Would she give him the chance to do that again? Could her heart take it?

She'd said enough while they were dancing, and had no desire to humiliate herself again, or set herself up for heartbreak.

"That's right, there is more going on," she averred. "There's you being very heavy-handed with me, don't you think?"

"I don't know what to think right now."

"That makes two of us."

He rubbed a hand over his face. "Dammit, Grace, I'm just trying to protect you."

"And I'm telling you I don't want or need your protection."

"Fine. Then there's nothing left for us to say."

He spun from the room and seconds later the front door slammed. A few seconds after that she heard Maren's cry: the noise had awakened her from her nap. Johanna's muffled voice filtered down from the upstairs. In a few moments they'd both be up and about, and Grace wanted to be gone before that happened. The last thing she needed was more questions.

Hastily she shoved the final check in an envelope and scribbled a quick note, putting it all in the center of the table. When she went out to her car, Mike was gone.

Men, she thought irrationally, slamming into the car and shoving it into gear. She was two miles down the road when something felt wrong. Grace pushed on the gas pedal, her eyes widening with alarm at the sudden loud clunk that shook the car. Everything seized... She cranked the wheel and her foot instantly hit the brake. Her head snapped forward, hitting the wheel just above her right eye.

She was finally stopped dead, square in the middle of the road. Her heart pounded so loudly she could hear it in her ears.

She couldn't just sit here. She shifted into park and then into drive again. Nothing. She could not move.

"No, no, no," she chanted, shifting again, desperate to get off the road. "Do *not* quit on me, baby."

Unfortunately, the vehicle wasn't listening, because it stubbornly stayed in the middle of the dirt road. She turned off the engine, unbuckled her seatbelt, and got out.

Something smelled hot. She got down on her hands and knees and looked underneath. Reddish-pink fluid dripped on to the ground.

Grace got up, dusting off her pants and taking several deep breaths. She was fine. This wasn't like the other time. The car was stopped but she was unhurt. She left the driver's side door opened, grabbed the wheel with one hand, and managed to push the hunk of metal a few feet closer to the shoulder of the road.

She hadn't gone off the road, hadn't hit anything. *It could be worse,* she reminded herself, knowing exactly how much worse it might have been. Panting from the exertion of pushing the car, she took a few moments to sit on the front bumper and catch her breath. Her hair was askew around her face, so she let it down all the way, letting it cascade over her shoulders.

Of all the things to happen today. First the cold, then fighting with Mike, twice even. Their arguing had to stop, and she had to come up with a way to get it through his thick head once and for all that she was running her own life. It had been much easier when he'd kept his distance, going about his business and just being the regular friend he'd always been.

Tears threatened. "Stop it," she chided herself. Just because she was tired and still a bit sick was no reason to get all emotional. And neither was Mike a reason. She got back up and lifted the hood, as if magically looking beneath it she'd figure out exactly what had gone wrong. Now that he seemed to be paying her more attention it was driving her crazy. But she'd asked for it, hadn't she? Asked for Mike to look at her differently.

She put the hood back down and sighed, remembering the feel of his fingers on her face, how close his lips had been to hers this afternoon. He was right. There was something between them.

But Mike was changing. He was settling down. He had his own business now and was building a house... Looking to the future, and probably a family. All the things she'd wanted back then.

For that very reason, there shouldn't be anything between them. Not if she were to be fair.

She grabbed her purse from the car and squinted up at the sun. At least there was no chance of rain. That would have been the icing on the cake. Her thin-soled sandals slapped on the light asphalt of the road as she started back toward the ranch. She'd have to go back and call for someone to tow the car. And who knew how much that would cost to fix. Her budget was already stretched too thin.

She was about a half mile from the vehicle when she saw a figure on horseback cutting through the pasture on her left. She kept walking. It could be any number of hands; she knew exactly how many because she'd written their checks that very afternoon.

The rider grew closer, astride a magnificent animal. She recognized the hat first, the horse second. It was Mike. And he was riding

Lightning, his black gelding with the distinctive crooked blaze running from forelock to nose. He trotted up, then slowed to a walk on the other side of the fence. She stared straight ahead, ignoring him.

"Trouble, Grace?" His smooth voice goaded her from across the fence.

"I'm out for my afternoon stroll," she replied dryly.

"I see. Car die?" He sat back in the saddle, resting one hand on a hard thigh.

Oh, duh, she thought. He knew darn well it had or she wouldn't be walking.

"I'm just going back to call the garage and get it towed."

"It's nearly two miles. And you're going to have blisters in those cute little things."

She stopped, gave him a withering glare, then reached down and slipped off the sandals, looping the straps jauntily around her index finger and walking again, barefoot.

Lightning followed, Mike's laughter echoing with that of a red-winged blackbird.

"I know you hate men coming to your rescue, and telling you what to do," he began.

She should be spitting mad after their arguments. She should be shaken by the close call she'd just had. She should not be feeling the corners of her mouth twitch, but a teasing Mike was horribly difficult to resist. Always had been.

"That would assume one would need rescuing," she countered, keeping her eyes on the road. If she looked him in the eyes now, he'd know he'd got to her, and she wasn't ready to give in. He'd get all proprietary again.

"But if you would allow me to offer you my assistance..."

Her lips quivered at his formal tone. He was incorrigible!

"Lightning and I would be happy to give you a lift back to the ranch."

She turned her head then, looking at him for the first time since he'd come up beside her.

She would always have a soft spot for Mike Gardner. Just looking at him, a little dusty, a whole lot man, astride his favorite horse...gray eyes crinkled around the edges with teasing while a smile flirted with the corners of his mouth...she couldn't resist.

Just this once.

"All right," she gave in. She slipped the sandals back on her feet and picked her way through the scratchy grass to the fence. Mike leaned over and lifted the top wire, making more space for her to crawl through. Once she was in the pasture she walked around Lightning's head, giving his forelock a little scratch as she went by.

"What happened to you?"

Suddenly Mike's voice changed and Grace looked up, confused. She was even more mystified when he leapt from the saddle, standing before her. "Are you all right?"

"Of course I am. Why wouldn't I be?"

Mike reached into his back pocket and pulled out a handkerchief. A hanky? she thought irrationally. Mike Gardner carried hankies?

He pushed her hair back with a commanding hand and touched the white cotton to her forehead. She winced with surprise at the pain.

"You didn't know?" His voice was low, soothing.

"I must have bumped my head."

"It's bleeding." He dabbed at the cut. "Mostly in your hair. What happened?"

"She died. Just a big clunk and she seized up right there."

She tried not to think of how gentle his hands were as he tended to her wound.

"A clunk? You must have lost your transmission." His fingers parted her hair, dabbing softly at the blood and enlarging bump.

"Maybe. It won't go anywhere. I tried putting it in gear, but nothing." She pushed his hands away, having had enough fussing and probing. "There was some red fluid underneath, if that tells you anything."

"Sure sounds like transmission fluid." Mike bent at the knees, peering into her face. "Can you ride? I'll help you up."

"I wasn't really hurt," she protested, putting her foot in the stirrup. She really didn't feel much of anything at all. She grabbed the saddle horn, Mike's hands strong at her waist as she took a hop and slid into the saddle. Once astride, she realized the stirrups were too long for her legs.

She thought maybe he'd lead Lightning back to the barn, which was far enough away now that it looked like a tiny shed dotting the prairie. But Mike put his boot in one stirrup, hoisted himself up, and sat behind her.

The saddle was big, but regardless it wasn't made for two people. Her backside was cushioned intimately in the vee of his thighs as she gave him back both the stirrups, the length set for his much longer legs. His right arm came around her, gripping the reins; his left wrapped around her waist, holding her firmly against him.

It was the closest she'd ever been to being in Mike's arms in several years and feeling him pressed against her sent memories flooding back. He was so close she could feel his heartbeat against her shoulder, the way the muscles in his legs cradled hers. As angry as she was with him, being tucked securely against his body did things to her. Arousing things. She'd been only seventeen when they'd tried dating, and her stomach had quivered then every time he'd touched her. Now was no different. Her heart beat a little faster, her body aware of every inch of contact.

"Hang on," he murmured in her ear, and the hair on the back of her neck prickled from the warmth of his breath.

He spurred Lightning and her breath caught in her chest as they took off at a rolling canter.

Her hair ruffled back from her face as she gripped the saddle horn, surprised by the jolt of the gait. And feeling more in danger than she had in a long time. A danger that had nothing to do with horses or cars but everything to do with a cowboy named Mike Gardner.

CHAPTER 4

Mike guided Lightning into the barn, the horse's hooves clopping steadily on the concrete floor. He dismounted, and Grace immediately felt the loss of his body pressed against hers. Wordlessly he dropped the reins, reached up, and helped her out of the saddle.

In that moment, had he leaned the slightest bit forward, she would have forgotten about all the reasons why he infuriated her and she would have kissed him. Put her lips against his just to see how it would feel; whether or not he still tasted the same as she remembered. It was the second time the urge had struck her that afternoon. His arms held her firmly as her feet touched the ground, but then he was gone, grabbing the reins again and leading Lightning down the corridor.

It was just as well. Grace took a restorative breath. She had to get up to the house anyway and call the garage. A heaviness filled her chest at the thought that the car couldn't be fixed. What would she do then? She couldn't afford a new one, not now. And repairs were sure to stretch her budget far out of capacity.

She'd probably been stupid to buy the house. She could have come back and rented a small one-bedroom apartment. It really was all she needed. Then there wouldn't be upkeep costs, insurance, property taxes...but after leaving Edmonton, she'd been fierce about her independence. She hadn't come through the divorce with much, but there had been enough for a down payment. Her little yellow bungalow was her defiant way of saying she could make it on her own.

She left Mike with the horse and went back out in the sunshine, heading toward the house with long strides. It didn't matter now. She *had* bought the house, and the car, and had brought her share of legal fees with her when she'd come back. Now she'd just have to find a way to make ends meet like she always did. The only one who could take care of her was *her*. She'd learned that the hard way. Twice now.

Phil answered the phone at Bob's Automotive when she called. Phil was Bob's son, but she still couldn't help but laugh every time she called and heard, "Bob's Automotive, Phil speaking." He promised he'd have someone pick up her car within the next hour.

She was hanging up when Mike came inside. "You get a tow?"

"I did. Phil's sending someone out."

"Great."

She moved past him and went outside on the narrow verandah. "Yeah, well, it's going to suck being without wheels. God knows how long it'll take to fix it."

He followed her back out the door. "If it's your transmission, and it sounds like it is, it could be a while."

Wonderful. Her shoulders drooped. How in the world was she supposed to pay for a whole new transmission?

Mike stepped forward, raising his hand and tenderly probing the bump on her forehead. "Seatbelts. Honestly, Grace. Are you sure you're okay?"

She shrugged off his touch and his criticism. "You, Mr. Concussion-from-too-many-saddlebroncs, you're going to lecture me about seatbelts? For your limited information, it was buckled. Knowing that old junker, it probably didn't function right. You don't need to beat it into me."

"You could have really been hurt if you'd actually gone off the road."

She turned to walk away but he reached out and caught her arm, pulling her back. "What if you have a concussion? Do you have a headache? Dizziness?"

His hand was still firm on her wrist, and she fought against the excitement thrumming through her veins. Her laugh was tight and strained as she countered.

"You're familiar with concussion symptoms, but I guess you should be after what, four? Five?" She tilted her chin. "The only thing giving me a headache today is *you.*"

The last thing she should have expected was for him to smile. But he did. A slow, make-your-heart-burn smile that crawled up his cheek.

"Grace, I don't ever remember it being this much fun to argue with you."

She pulled away and put her hands on her hips, because she knew if she didn't, she'd wipe that smirk off his face with her lips. She simply had to stop thinking about kissing him! "Maybe because you didn't stay around long enough to find out."

His grin faded. It was the desired outcome, but it made her feel small for using it.

"Don't mind me. I have bigger concerns at the moment, thank you." She didn't intend for it to come out as coolly as it did.

Mike's chin flattened and he stared over her shoulder. "Don't worry about your car. I'll take care of it."

He'd what? Grace stiffened.

Second verse, third, fourth and fifth, same as the first. The man was unbelievable. When was he going to realize she didn't want to be taken care of?

"I'm perfectly capable, thank you just the same." She said the words through gritted teeth.

"Hey, you were out here working for Circle M. The least I can do is take care of fixing your car. Come to think of it, if you're without transportation, you can borrow one of the farm trucks."

"Here's a newsflash." She tossed her head. Darn it, it *was* starting to ache after all. The fact that he was right—about her head, about her seatbelt, only made her more annoyed. "I don't want, nor do I need, your help." For a moment she swayed. In a flash, the adrenaline from the near-miss drained from her and she started to shake. She could have been hurt again, and the realization slammed into her. She knew that fear, that shock of an eternity happening in a split second. Grace put her hands on the railing and tried deep breaths to gain control over her trembling.

She heard an engine approaching, wondering if it was Phil with the tow truck. Instead, Connor's truck was coming up the drive, swirling up dust.

"Look at you. You're shaking like a leaf." He came up behind her, rested a large palm on her back. His voice gentled. "Why are you so set on never letting anyone help you? Why do you have to do everything yourself?"

Mike wouldn't understand. He'd always done exactly what he wanted, when he wanted to do it. And that included leaving her behind. She'd hated being in town so much after he was gone that she'd rashly decided to go to Red Deer to college.

It had been a big mistake, and one she tried to forget so she didn't waste her energy with regret. Mike hadn't had choices taken away from him in the blink of an eye. The reason her heart had pounded so heavily when her car had skidded to a stop was from sheer fright. In that split second that she lost control, she relived her accident all over again.

Even now, with her delayed reaction happening long minutes after it was over, she relived the pain, the fear of being in the hospital, the devastation of waking up from surgery to the horrific news.

She knew why she was so independent. She'd trusted Mike, and when he wasn't there anymore, she'd relied on a substitute to make things right, and it had only gone wrong. She had acknowledged long ago that she'd been young and had tried to replace Mike by finding someone else. She wouldn't make the same mistakes again.

But he didn't know about her earlier accident. And she wasn't going to be the one to tell him and make herself even more pathetic in his eyes. She pulled away from his touch.

"Stop being such a Neanderthal and wake up to the fact that we're in the twenty-first century. Women are fully capable of looking after themselves. I don't need you, Mike."

His face changed, blanked completely. "Then how do you intend on getting home, then? Fly?"

Oh Lord, she hadn't thought of that. It seemed she did need him after all.

Connor's truck door slammed. Before Mike could blink, she turned and leaned over the rail, smiling sweetly.

"Connor? I've had some car trouble. Would you mind driving me home?"

She saw Connor's glance flicker to Mike and hold for a moment. She didn't need to turn around to know Mike was staring stonily ahead. She didn't hold the franchise on being stubborn.

"Mike could…"

"Oh, I don't want to trouble Mike. He already brought me back and made sure I was all right." She turned on the charm. "I just need a lift back to my house, and I can see to getting everything set right."

"Well, okay." He looked up again at Mike. "Tell Alex I'll be back in half an hour, will you?"

Mike didn't answer, just turned on a booted heel and went inside, slamming the screen door behind him. Grace climbed into the cab of the truck, shut the door, and fastened her seatbelt. Connor stood in the middle between the house and the truck for a moment, before getting in the vehicle and starting the engine.

·•••••••••·

Grace hesitated outside the glass and metal door of Bob's Automotive. Through the window she could see her poor sedan up on the hoist. She was scared half to death to hear what Phil had to say. She couldn't afford to replace her car even though she knew she should. At least Phil would let her take her car when it was done and let her pay a little each week until her bill was settled. It was one of the benefits of living in the town where you grew up.

She opened the glass-and-metal door and went inside. Instantly she was greeted by the grinding screech of air tools and coarse shouts of mechanics.

Phil caught sight of her standing by the front counter and approached, wiping his hands on a rag. "Morning, Grace," he greeted.

"Hey, Phil." She nodded towards the car. "It's not good, is it."

"You lost your transmission."

Her heart sank. Transmissions were bad. Very, very bad. She'd had a feeling, and remembered Mike commenting on the possibility, but she'd hoped it was something easier like a cracked hose.

"Is it worth fixing?"

"Well, you could buy another older model, but then there wouldn't be any guarantee it wouldn't do the same thing. Best thing I can do is replace it for you. I can have a look around for a cheaper, used one. But you've still got labor on top of that."

Naturally. She took a breath and held it. "Total damage?"

"A couple of thousand. Should be able to do it all up for under twenty-five hundred."

Twenty-five hundred dollars. Right now, it might as well be twenty-five thousand. Her breath came out in a rush. Would she never catch a break?"And how long?"

"Next Wednesday? Take me a few days to get a new one in, and we're swamped."

"Okay. Thanks Phil."

She turned to walk back out the door when his voice stopped her. "Hey, Grace?"

"Yeah?" She looked over her shoulder. Phil looked genuinely sorry. He was ten years older than Grace, but his little sister had gone to school with her.

"Mike called in yesterday. We've already had a look at your seatbelt, and it's fixed. And if it's money that's got you panicked, don't worry. He said Circle M is going to cover it, since it happened while you were on the job."

Every nerve ending in her body prickled. How dare he go around her, go to Phil and just announce that he was paying for everything! After their conversation! She felt heat rise up her chest and neck, settling in her cheeks.

Her fingers tightened on the metal bar of the door, gripping until her knuckles turned white.

"Phil, the last I checked, the registration for that hunk of junk is in my name. Which means I pay for repairs. Under no circumstances do you talk to Mike Gardner, you hear? Circle M is *not* paying for a new transmission or any other maintenance. Period."

"Yes ma'am." Phil paused for a moment, then cleared his throat. "If money's an issue anyway, we can work something out. We'll just put it on an account and you can pay a little every month. I know you're good for it."

Tears stung her eyes and she blinked them back. For a while she'd considered staying in Edmonton, living in the city and going back to school. But at moments like this, she knew she'd done the right thing coming back.

"Thanks, Phil," she answered. She went back outside into the fall sunshine, burning with humiliation. What in the world was Mike trying to do, anyway? He had to know she'd never agree to such a plan.

As much as she hated to do it, she was going to have to find another job. And pray that somehow there ended up being a few extra hours in the day so she could get some sleep.

· · · ● ● · ● ● ● · ·

Grace covered her mouth, stifling a yawn. At least the bookwork had gone smoothly. It hadn't taken long to catch up. The checks were written according to the invoices, the envelopes were made up, and she was just waiting for signatures. Connor and Mike were both out in the fields, thankfully. Johanna was on her way out for groceries, and Maren was sleeping. She heard the faint sound of the television from upstairs: Alex was watching a daytime show.

The bed rest had to be driving Alex crazy. Grace looked at her watch. She'd make them both a cup of tea and have a visit. Lately there'd been lots of times she'd wished she could just lay in bed, but she knew without a doubt that if she had to be there, like Alex was now, she'd be climbing the walls. When she finally shut the computer down, she heard giggles coming from upstairs. Maren was awake.

Grace made tea, grabbed a juice box from the fridge, and went upstairs.

Maren snuggled Alex on the bed, her head resting against the growing mound of Alex's tummy. Absently Alex played with Maren's dark curls, twirling them around her index finger as a children's show flickered on the TV screen, holding Maren's attention.

It was a scene that Grace knew she'd never have, and she swallowed against the bittersweet lump in her throat.

Alex turned and caught her standing in the doorway. "Grace! Come on in!"

Grace stepped inside. "I brought tea."

"Here, honey, slide down here. Mama's going to have something hot."

"Hotttt." Maren repeated the word.

"She's really starting to talk." Grace handed Alex a mug.

"Don't I know it. Babbles all day."

She put her tea on the bedside table and then inserted the straw into the juice box for Maren. Once the toddler was settled, Grace perched on the edge of the bed.

"So, how're you doing?"

Alex sighed. "I'm sick and tired of being in bed, sick and tired of being pregnant, sick and tired of not being able to do anything. I'm not even supposed to pick up my own daughter."

When Grace met Alex's eyes, she was dismayed to see tears glimmering in the corners.

"I'm sorry," she offered. "You just need to get out of this room."

Alex's frustration was clear and understandable, Grace thought as she sipped her tea. She looked at Alex, dressed in maternity yoga pants and a baggy sweatshirt. What the woman needed was to feel like a *woman* again. Maybe she could help with that. First had to be getting her dressed. In something nicer than an old sweatshirt of Connor's.

"You need a girlie day."

Alex snorted. "Yeah, right. I'm not allowed to go anywhere."

"So what? I'll bring it to you."

She went to the bathroom and got out a brush, a makeup bag, nail polish, and a bag of hair accessories.

While Maren watched, wide eyed, Grace gently got Alex changed into a pair of maternity jeans and a cute red jersey top with long, slender sleeves. Once she was reclined on the bed once more, Grace picked up the brush and starting brushing out Alex's long, black hair. She and Alex had become friends since Alex had moved to Windover, but the intimate gesture of brushing her hair seemed to solidify their growing affection more than anything previous.

"So, what's happening between you and Mike?"Grace felt the blush heat her cheeks, knew it was truly bad when the outsides of her ears burned. "Nothing."

Alex laughed, pointing to Grace's face. "Girls don't blush like that over nothing. You've been fighting like cats and dogs."

"He's just gotten overprotective lately." Grace dismissed the comment, focusing on Alex's hair. She gathered it up and began plaiting it into a loose French braid.

"There's something. I can feel it, even being up here away from everyone."

Grace met Alex's eyes in the mirror, her hands still plaiting blindly as she grabbed the opportunity to change the subject. Alex had to know she and Mike had been an item once, and Grace didn't want it to come up. "It's been horrid for you, hasn't it?"

"I just keep reminding myself what the payoff will be. That's what really matters."

Hair finished, Grace took out polish and went to work on Alex's feet. Alex smiled, wiggling her red toes. "Thank you, Grace. I needed this today."

"Nonsense. Connor leaves you up here all day, while he gets to go off and do all his *stuff*. Men," she muttered.

Alex laughed. "So he *is* getting to you."

"Hah. Mike Gardner is way too big for his britches, running around thinking he can tell everyone what to do. What is it about men that make them think they can just park us somewhere and we'll do exactly what we're told?"

Alex's lips twitched and she patted the mound of her belly. "They do come in handy sometimes."

Grace ran a hand through her hair. "Yeah. Handy. Look at this gorgeous fall day. It's fifteen degrees out and it smells like fall, and you're stuck here in bed. You've got a balcony out there, for Pete's sake!"

Abruptly she stood up. "You know what? You sit here. I have an idea."

She reached into the bag of hair accessories and pulled out an elastic and a scrunchie. "Today you're going to enjoy the outdoors, and we don't need a man to do it."

Grace stomped down the stairs, putting in a ponytail as she went. At the bottom she paused, twisting the tail around and around and anchoring it to the back of her head with the scrunchie—a cheater bun. *Stupid men. Poor Alex up there day in and day out on bed rest.*

She went out on to the back deck. The swing was too big; she'd never be able to move it alone. And regular patio chairs weren't that comfortable at the best of times, and she couldn't imagine how they'd feel to a heavily pregnant woman. But the other chair—she could manage that. She took the cushions off first and marched them upstairs.

"What are you doing?" Alex called after her as she hit the stairs again.

"You'll see," she shouted back.

Getting the furniture upstairs was another matter. It was a light metal frame, about the length of a loveseat with a back on it. Alex could stretch out if she wanted, or simply tuck herself into the corner and enjoy the fresh air. It was big enough she could share it with Maren, or with Connor.

Grace got the contraption into the kitchen and through the wide doorway to the hall. Getting it around the corner of the stairs was nearly impossible, and Grace was terrified she'd slip and take a piece out of the woodwork. Panting, she took it one step at a time, cringing every time she heard the metal legs bang against the stair risers ahead. She was almost at the top when it slipped. She scrambled to catch it, saving it just in time from hitting the solid wood banister, but catching the side of her hand on a screw. She bit down on her lip to keep from cursing.

Getting it through the bedroom meant lifting the frame over the bed, then dragging it through the sliding doors that led to the balcony.

Once the seat was in place, Grace wiped her glistening brow and arranged the cushions. "Don't go out yet," she cautioned. "There's more."

She went back downstairs and retrieved a small table that Alex could use to set a drink on, or a book. The next trip revealed the huge snake plant from the study, which Grace placed in a corner, and a soft chenille blanket for when she might get a chill now that fall had settled in for good.

When it was done, she was red and sweating, pieces of hair dangling messily along the sides of her face, but with a triumphant smile.

"There. Now you can come out."

Alex moved gingerly, as she always did these days, settling herself in the seat and sighing.

"Connor should have seen to this long ago."

Alex smiled wistfully. "Don't blame Connor. He's been so preoccupied."

Grace sighed. "I know. But honestly, men just don't see the little things."

"But you did. Thank you so much, Grace." Maren scrambled up beside her mother, carrying a stuffed cat and a book. "Oh, dear, you're bleeding!" Alex pointed at Grace's hand.

Sure enough, she was. She must have done it when the frame slipped. She hoped she didn't get any blood on the cushions. "It's just a scratch."

"There's first aid stuff in the bathroom downstairs. Oh, Grace."

Grace fluttered her other hand. "Don't worry about it. A band-aid and it'll be fine. You just enjoy what's left of the morning."

Grace was downstairs in the bathroom washing her hand when she heard the front door open. Booted feet paused, then went upstairs. Moments later they clattered back down.

Please, let it be Connor.

No such luck.

"What in the world were you thinking?"

She grabbed a band-aid from the box and turned to face Mike, regarding him blandly. "Good morning, Mike."

"You carried that stuff up there all by yourself?"

"I did. I'm not helpless, as you seem to think." She peeled the wrapping off the bandage and stuck the first tab on her hand.

"Helpless? You? Never. You have the temper of a snake."

She laughed. Finally. Maybe, just maybe she was finally getting through to him. He'd changed clothes, she realized. He looked far too neat and tidy for a man who'd been out working for hours already. His T-shirt was brown and hugged his shoulders, and his jeans were unblemished.

"Going somewhere?"

"What?" He furrowed his brow at her.

"Clean jeans, tidy shirt. I know you didn't do that just for me, Mike." She let her lips curve on one side, and she raised an eyebrow in his direction.

For a moment he didn't say anything, and Grace got the giddy feeling she might have actually managed to embarrass him a little.

"I got thrown."

She couldn't help it, she snorted. "I see."

"Stupid colt. Scared of his own shadow." Mike shoved his hands in his pockets.

Grace laughed. "Kind of makes you realize why you stopped the circuit, huh. Saddlebronc riders that get thrown by colts don't really hit pay dirt. Just the dirt."

"I'm glad you find it funny."

She finished sticking the band aid to her hand, giving it an extra pat. "I do, actually. Since you're still in one piece and all."

"So are you going to tell me why, exactly, you're bleeding?"

"Alex has been stuck in that room day in and day out. She wanted to get some fresh air and sunshine. What's she doing now?"

Mike lowered his voice. "She's snuggled up with Maren, the two of them under the blanket, reading stories."

Grace smiled. "Oh, that's lovely."

Mike came forward and took her wrist in his hand. "You cut yourself. If you'd waited, I would have helped you take that seat upstairs."

"I didn't know when anyone would be coming back in, and I knew I could do it myself."

He took a second bandage and applied it to the rest of the cut on her hand. Having Mike doctor her so tenderly did things to her insides. If he'd stop being so bossy, maybe he'd see what was right in front of him. She frowned. That idea had complications of its own.

"You don't have to do everything by yourself," he countered. "I talked to Phil today. He said you refused to let me pay anything on your account."

"Of course I did."

"Why?"

She pulled her hand away. "Because I pay my own way. I live my own life. I make my own decisions. I...I don't rely on other people."

She didn't, not anymore. Other people disappointed. Mike had disappointed her. Steve had let her down. It was far better to look after yourself and deal with those consequences.

"I know something about that," he answered.

"Yes, you do. And why do you make your own choices?"

His eyes met hers squarely. "Because relying on other people means eventually you'll be disappointed."

"That's right." She took a breath, finally challenging him. "People let other people down. You won't let anyone dictate your life. So why do you try to do it to me?"

"Because...because...oh damn." He scowled. "Because you constantly seem to need it!"

Grace stepped back. That was what he thought of her then. Still the girl who couldn't look after herself.

She pressed her fingers to her eyes, worn out. Tears threatened but she held them back. For weeks she'd been working long hours, and fighting with Mike so much lately drained her more than she'd cared to admit. Seeing Alex pregnant, her family around her, caused Grace so much hurt it actually pained her physically. All the things she wanted—security, love, a family of her own—never had they seemed so far away. She wanted to lift her chin and say something scathing, but for once it wasn't in her.

"You gave up the right to that a long time ago," she murmured. "And I'm tired of fighting." She tried to swallow the tears that clogged her throat. "I can't do it anymore, Mike. Just leave me alone."

CHAPTER 5

Mike took a step closer, putting his large hand on Grace's shoulder. "I'm sorry," he murmured. "I didn't mean to make you cry."

She sniffled, gaining control. "You didn't. I'm not crying. It's just everything has been piling up. I'm fine, really."

"You're not fine. You just said so."

She didn't have an answer to that. He was right. She'd asked to be left alone because she couldn't take the constant pressure from him anymore.

"I just need to take a break. That's all."

What she really wanted to do was rest against his solid strength. As infuriating as his overprotectiveness had been lately, the one thing she'd always known in her heart was that she could count on him. Even after he left her, she knew if she were in trouble, she could call and he'd be there. There weren't many people she could say that about. She sighed and leaned back into his hand. Even that much was a comfort. A feeling that for a few moments she wasn't alone.

Her back was still to him, and she closed her eyes as he squeezed her shoulder. "There's more to this than just being tired, isn't there?"

Grace swallowed against the lump in her throat. Mike's hand left her shoulder and his arms came around her, pulling her back against his chest. He said nothing else, just held her for a few minutes. She wished she could give him more. She wasn't the only one who needed a break. She knew he'd been working too hard himself, running the bulk of the ranch now as well as overseeing the building of his house. Like her, he didn't have family close by to rely on. He was carrying his own weight and a lot of Connor's as well. She knew he didn't mind it in the least, but it didn't mean he wasn't tired or stressed out.

Reluctantly she pulled out of his arms and turned to face him. "Thank you," she murmured softly. "I needed that. I'm sorry, too. I've jumped down your throat lately when all you've been doing is trying to help."

"Let's get out of here," he suggested. "Let's forget about the arguments. Come with me and I'll show you how the house is coming along."

She had work waiting for her at home and a shift at the tavern that night, but it couldn't hurt to take a half hour and go with him. She wanted to spend time with him, she admitted to herself. It had been a long time since they'd spent time together that had no purpose other than to escape everyday pressures. And she *was* curious about the house. Every time she came out to the ranch, she saw changes. First the basement, then the frame. Now the roof was on and there were holes for windows and doors. She'd thought he'd build a regular two-story house, something like Windover. Instead, the building that was forming was a low ranch-style that turned a corner. She wondered what it would be like inside.

"That sounds nice. I'd love to see it."

The house sat northeast of Connor's, a rough gravel drive leading to it off the main ranch road. As they started past the barns, Grace saw two white pickups driving away toward the main road.

"Lunch time, I guess," Mike commented as they walked side by side. Grace looked up at the house, admiring. It sat on top of a small knoll, and she had a feeling the view of the mountains from the west windows would be spectacular.

The late morning remained cool, and Grace tucked her arms around her even though she wore a thick sweater. Mike had thrown a jacket over his t-shirt, a rich brown that set off the coppery tones in his hair. He'd always had a way about him, long strides that covered ground without being hurried, a quiet assurance that he always knew exactly what he was doing. As they approached the house, he took her hand to lead her over the uneven spots. Grace hesitated a moment, captivated by the feel of her smaller hand in his. Then he tugged, helping her over the mounds of uneven dirt to the front entrance.

Even without paint, or windows, or furniture, she was enthralled. It had a feeling about it. It was large, but the design was intimate. She wandered from room to room, her footsteps shuffling against the wood and dust inside, sidestepping occasionally around tools left by the workmen. She went down a wide hall and discovered bedrooms on the east side. At the very end was a huge room with a smaller one off it. It was the frame for the master bedroom and what she could only assume would be a private ensuite.

She went back down the hall and found Mike standing in front of a huge opening, facing the mountains. They were visible in the clear autumn air, their white-tipped peaks a sharp contrast to the brilliant blue of the September sky.

"You're going to love it here."

Without looking at her, he answered. "My first home. Can you believe that? Over thirty, and I've never had my own place."

"It's going to be beautiful," she answered, her eyes on the same view as his. "You picked a great spot. Far enough away from Windover to be private, yet still on ranch land. And I can tell the house is going to be great. I can see the design and everything already." She could picture low tables, cozy couches, and warm lamps in the living room. Maybe a television in the corner, and a comfortable chair where Mike would kick back with a beer at the end of a long day.

"I never thought I'd want to be tied down. But somehow...I guess I grew up."

She laughed lightly. Goodness, Mike wasn't getting sentimental, was he? All philosophical? These lapses really made it quite difficult for her to stay angry with him. Yet at the same time, she remembered wanting to give him this type of security long ago and how he'd run from it. She couldn't help but resent it just a bit.

"It happens to all of us sometime. Just takes longer for others, I guess."

She'd done her growing up long ago. Out of necessity.

He stepped away from the window and wandered to the next large room which she assumed was the kitchen. She pictured him sitting at a table all by himself with a setting for one, eating dinner in the winter dark. It was a lonely picture indeed.

"Do you even know how to cook?" she teased from where she stood, her voice echoing through the open space.

He laughed. "Not really. Unless bacon and eggs counts."

She knew what was in store for him. She lived alone and had for several years. No one to fight for the remote, or who ate something you'd set aside for later, or leaving their wet towels on the bathroom floor.

No one to talk to, to share a meal with, to watch a movie with a bowl of popcorn between you. Living alone was a horribly solitary existence.

But it wasn't like she'd ever be living with Mike, either. Even without the complications she would bring to a relationship, she already knew how he felt about her. They'd been friends too long. He cared about her; she knew that. He always had. But if Connor weren't so concerned for Alex right now, he would have acted the same way toward Grace. Like an older brother. All the other atmosphere between them was only a product of her own imaginings and a case of dwelling on sweet memories best forgotten.

"Where'd you go?"

Her head snapped up. He was standing close, too close. Her body warmed just from having him there, only an arm's length away. He was big and hulking in his heavy jacket, his cheeks ruddy from the brisk air. It wasn't fair for him to look so gorgeous when she was already fantasizing about him.

"Just thinking."

She turned away, but his hand on her arm stopped her from moving. "Don't run away."

"I'm not."

"Grace, you've been running away for years."

He sure picked a great time to finally get observant, she noted with irritation. "I don't know what you mean."

"Sure you do." His face told her he knew better. "What I don't get is why. Why do you work so hard to keep people at arm's length, when you obviously care very much about them? Everyone knows you and loves you. You're the town sweetheart. You do so much for people, yet I don't think any of them can say they know what makes you tick." He didn't know the secrets she held so closely guarded either. And if he did, she knew he'd look at her differently. She didn't want to see the look in his eyes when he realized what a disappointment she was. Even as she craved to be touched, to be loved by him again, she knew he wouldn't see her in the same way if he knew the truth. And she knew he'd run, just as he had before. She couldn't face that kind of hurt again.

But her secret was a burden she carried every day, and the more they argued, the more he showed his protective nature, the more she longed to finally let it out and be free of it.

"And you're gone again."

She shook her head, staring up into his eyes. There was no censure there, not this time. Instead there was just concern, and an edge of something else. It almost looked like desire. But no, that would be her fancies carrying her away again. He didn't think of her that way, she reminded herself.

"Mike..."

He was so close the zipper of his jacket was pressing against her sweater. Gently he placed a rough finger beneath her chin, tilting it up until her eyes met his. Automatically her gaze dropped to his lips, and she was mesmerized as they pursed slightly as he whispered, "Shhhh."

Her breath caught; her heart stopped for an ethereal moment. Then he put his lips on hers and everything coursed through her in a rush.

At last. Every pore in her body seemed to breathe those two words as her eyes drifted closed. Mike let go of her chin and instead put his hands on her arms, just above her elbows, pulling her closer. His lips teased, coaxed with the lightest of touches. He wasn't pushing, she suddenly realized. He was being careful with her. Knowing it touched her heart, but she didn't need him to be careful. She just needed *him.*

She opened her lips a little wider in invitation. Carefully he deepened the kiss, like he was testing to see how she'd respond. She finally did what she'd wanted to do since the night they'd danced and she embarrassed herself. She lifted her arms and threaded her fingers through his hair, pulling his head down and putting everything she could offer into the kiss. She wanted him, wanted to know she could make him lose control, wanted to know she made him want her as much as she wanted him.

Once she made it clear what she was asking, everything changed.

He broke off the kiss, took command. His gaze burned into hers and excitement raced to her every extremity like an electric current. He was suddenly bigger, stronger. Forceful, which she didn't fear but welcomed. Demanding. His wide hand cupped the back of her neck even as his body pushed her backward until her movement was stopped by the two-by-six stud of the living room wall.

Mike's legs spread wide, and he pinned her there, taking her mouth completely.

He moaned, the sound vibrating in his throat, filling her with wonder. It had been nearly a decade since she'd last kissed him, but the taste of him was as familiar as if it had been yesterday. She was fortunate that he had her pressed so firmly against the wood because she knew that otherwise she'd be melted in one delicious puddle of ecstasy. Instead, she wilted, letting her body twine around him, filling all the lees between them.

When it seemed they couldn't possibly go on any longer in that position, Mike drew away. "Grace," he murmured. His hand slid from behind her head to her face, his wide fingers delicately brushing the pale skin of her cheekbone. Disbelief assaulted her as that gentle hand left her face and caressed the soft skin of her neck, slowly inching downwards, tracing a line through the middle of her chest. She watched, holding her breath, as his eyes seductively followed the path of his fingers. In a moment she knew he'd be touching her in all the places she longed to be touched by him. And she knew in that same suspended moment that it wouldn't be fair. To either of them.

She closed her eyes. "Stop," she said, huskily in the quiet of the empty house.

"You don't mean that."

When she looked up, he still wasn't looking at her, but watching his fingers as they moved on her body, a small smile playing on his lips. She swallowed, yearning for him to continue but desperate to stop before things went too far to turn back.

"Please, Mike, you need to stop." She inhaled and squared her shoulders. "We can't do this. We don't want the same things."

Mike's jaw hardened as he felt her pull away. Didn't want the same things? He knew they wanted each other; that much was perfectly plain.

But neither did he want to rush things and ruin it. Grace had been right about one thing today—she was getting worn out from spreading herself too thin. He didn't need to add to her stress. He wanted to help her, look out for her. He wanted all sorts of things for her, and he couldn't rush them.

"I'm sorry."

"Don't be. It just can't go any further, that's all."

She was avoiding looking at him and he wondered if he'd been wrong after all. She'd come on to him that night at the party, but she'd had a few drinks and had been goaded on by her friends. That didn't mean she was crazy about him. In fact, they'd been fighting most of the time lately. Maybe he'd misread her feelings. For a moment he felt exactly like he had every time the social worker told him he was moving again. Expendable. Not exactly what people had in mind as a "keeper." He knew what happened when he let himself love. He always got hurt. When they'd been seeing each other, he'd been the one to go so that she wouldn't be the one doing the leaving.

He backed away. "I don't want to pressure you into anything." He sensed her relief and couldn't resist adding, "But I'm not sorry, either."

The look she gave him was so complicated he didn't even try to interpret it. What conclusion could he possibly reach when her face was such a contradiction of arousal, hope, fear, and resignation? Nothing made sense. It should have been easy. Either she wanted him, or she didn't.

"We don't want the same things," she repeated.

"What does that mean?" Looking down into her eyes, he sensed she meant something far deeper than the raw need he was feeling right now.

She straightened her sweater and put on a regular smile. "I have to get back," she evaded. "Thank you for showing me your house."

He reached out and grabbed her arm. "Wait."

She looked up at him, silently begging him to let her go. He could see it in her eyes. But he persisted because after all this time it needed saying.

"I left you before without a word. And Grace, for that I'm truly sorry."

He saw her swallow, and her gaze dropped to between her feet.

"Forget it."

"Grace. I can't forget it after what just happened. Because if we're in danger of starting something again, we need to clear the air. You need to know that I was scared then and unfair to you. I wouldn't do that to you again."

He thought his words would reassure her, but instead her lips thinned, almost as if she were in pain.

"Thank you for the apology," she replied, her voice soft, as if she didn't trust it. "But it doesn't matter now, because we aren't starting anything. I need to get back."

It made him inexplicably angry, but he let her walk away rather than drag her into another fight. His body was still humming with the energy of their kiss. Not starting anything? Hah!

They'd already started plenty.

• • • • • • • • • •

Mike pocketed the truck keys and ran his fingers through his hair before putting his hat back on. Even from outside, he heard the rough beat of country music coming from the hotel tavern.

She was in there. *Working.*

He'd come across that tidbit of information quite by accident. Connor had stopped for some takeout as a treat for Alex one evening, and Grace had come in for her shift. It had taken two days for the topic to come up in conversation and it had been Alex who'd finally brought it up. He was sitting down with a couple of Johanna's cookies when she'd remarked on his foul mood and suggested a night out might put him in a better frame of mind.

He put his hand on the door handle. It had been a set-up, pure and simple. He'd seen it on Alex's face as she casually dropped the hint that he could see Grace while he was there.

This, then, was how she was paying for the repairs on her car. It bugged him knowing she'd rather be a barmaid than take his assistance. And the tavern was so rough.

He lowered his hat, shadowing his eyes, and walked in.

The light was dim, the noise nearly deafening as he made his way to the bar. She hadn't seen him come in, he realized, taking a stool. She was at the end of the bar, pouring a glass of whatever was on tap, laughing at something a customer said. They traded glass for money, and she turned.

When she saw him, her face soured. He met the look squarely as she came to take his order.

"Beer, Mike?"

The question was carefully casual, but Mike felt the coolness. He remembered all too well how she'd felt in his arms, how she'd tasted in his mouth. All it took was seeing her again to bring it all back. The way she looked tonight didn't help either. Her low-slung jeans were worn in all the right places and sat on her hips, while her t-shirt clung to her ribs like a second skin.

"Yeah. In the bottle."

She raised one eyebrow in his direction; in his nasty mood he hadn't even said please. And he'd be damned if he'd backtrack now.

When he said nothing, she turned away and leaned over to retrieve his brand from the cooler. As she did, the hem of her T-shirt slid up, the waistband of her jeans down, and he saw the delectable hollow of her back.

He wet his lips, but before he could contemplate it further, she brought his bottle, placed it on a plain white cocktail napkin in front of him. "You starting a tab?"

"I'll pay as I go," he responded, standing to dig his wallet out of his pocket while she waited. He handed her a five and said, "Keep it."

She tucked it into her apron. "You hungry? Jack's running the kitchen tonight so it's edible."

"Not right now."

She turned to leave.

"What are you doing here, anyway?"

She smiled at him, but he could tell it wasn't sincere. "I'm working, what does it look like?"

"But why here?"

She came closer so they wouldn't have to shout over the voices and music, and to keep their conversation private from other patrons. "Because the tips are good, and the schedule works with my other jobs, that's why."

"Surely you could have found something better than this."

He'd gone and offended her again; he could tell by the way her eyes narrowed slightly. "It's temporary. One of the waitresses is on holiday for a few weeks. The timing was right and it was too good to pass up."

"But you wouldn't have to do it at all if you'd let me help."

"Hey Grace! I'm dyin' of thirst over here!"

The call came from a local and Mike's eyes narrowed as she laughed good-naturedly in response. "Keep your shirt on Joe, I'm coming."

She was better than this, Mike thought as he nursed his beer, watching her work the room. She didn't need to be working day and night and negotiating such a tough crowd. Lord, this was the roughest establishment in town. He should know. He'd spent many an evening here over the years.

He couldn't take his eyes off her. He noticed she always had a smile for everyone. Everyone but him, it seemed. She delivered platters of fries and burgers and baskets of chicken wings, carted countless trays of beer and the other local staple, rye and coke. As the evening drew on, he ordered another beer, threatened by her admonishment of "order something or give your stool to a paying customer". The noise grew louder, the crowd more raucous. At the table behind him, he picked up bits and pieces of the conversation, and he didn't like it. It was all innuendoes and testosterone mixed with alcohol. As long as they were there, Mike decided, he wasn't leaving Grace here alone.

"Hey Grace, come to think of it, maybe I will have a steak sandwich."

She put the order in without saying anything. Both she and the other waitress, Pam, were hustling around trying to keep everyone fed and watered. She took the order of the table behind him, and when she went to the kitchen to place it he heard one of the men say, "Man, she's hot. The things I could do with a little filly like that."

Like hell, Mike scowled, growing angrier by the minute. This is what she put up with? The idiot that had spoken was no more than a randy kid who thought far too much of himself.

Grace delivered Mike's sandwich and smiled tightly. "I had Jack add hot sauce."

For the first time, he genuinely smiled back, surprised she'd remembered such a tiny detail about him after all their years apart.

"Thanks for remembering."

"I've known you a long time, Mike. Have you forgotten that?"

Of course he hadn't. Grace, even as a teenager, had always been kind and giving. She'd never thought less of him because of his upbringing. In a world where he'd constantly been someone's add-on, she'd always taken him exactly as he was. She'd been there for him and he'd cared more about her than he ever had anyone. Which was why he'd run in the first place. Caring that much had scared the living hell out of him.

He caught her hand before she could leave again. "You know I haven't forgotten. I can always count on you, Grace."

Her smile faltered and he wondered what he'd said wrong.

"I'll be back," she promised, pulling her hand away.

He cut into his steak, all the while his radar was tuned to the men sitting behind him. Grace delivered a tray of drinks. "Here, honey, you keep the change." A couple of snickers. "And how's about you let me buy you breakfast tomorrow?"

Mike put down his steak knife and spun a hundred and eighty degrees on his stool, lowering his head and staring down at the loudmouth. The man that had spoken was maybe twenty-two, twenty-three, with dusty boots and a belt buckle the size of a hubcap.

When Grace simply pocketed the cash, saying nothing, the laughter died down. Mike turned back to his sandwich as Grace walked back to the bar.

"Hey, I meant it about breakfast, baby," the guy called. "There's an extra twenty in it for you."

That was going too far. Even the innuendo of exchanging money for favours had Mike seeing red. Not his Grace. She wasn't that kind of woman and never would be. Mike stepped off his stool, walked over to the table, and calm-as-you please, gripped the collar of the offender's shirt and lifted him clean out of his chair. "You just don't know when to shut up," he cautioned calmly.

Conversations halted. The music kept blaring, but it sounded out of place in the room now devoid of laughter and chatter. It couldn't be any clearer that this group was passing through. Anyone in town knew better than to provoke Mike. His temper had a long fuse, but when it blew it was like fireworks. And right now, everyone was watching to see the show.

Mike simply held the man up so that his toes barely touched the floor and stared him down.

"Hey, sorry, bud," he said. "Didn't mean to poach."

Mike waited a few seconds, then let him down by slow inches. He felt Grace's eyes on him but didn't care. Grace wasn't a buckle bunny out for an eight-second ride. And this piece of scum had basically suggested she was the equivalent of a prostitute. If they weren't in a room full of people it would be a different story, but Mike held a thin rein on his temper.

When he turned he saw Grace staring at him, her face pale and eyes wide with something like fear and gratitude. It hit him so hard he felt like he always did the moment he got bucked off, suspended and waiting to hit the hard ground of the rodeo infield. Good lord, when had he fallen for her so hard? Right now, in this moment, he knew he'd do whatever it took to protect her. Knew if nothing else he wanted her to be *his*. Her words... "we don't want the same things..." rushed through his brain and he finally was certain of what he'd suspected all along. He did want those things. To settle down, make a home. To finish his house, living in it with her. The thing he'd never had going from foster home to foster home. And the staggering realization that it didn't scare him anymore. Well, he'd be damned.

Behind him more words reached his ears.

"Hey, I can't blame the guy. If I had a piece of tail that sweet, I wouldn't give it up either."

He sent Grace a brief look of apology before spinning and delivering a single, punishing punch.

CHAPTER 6

The chair behind the man crashed to the floor as he back flipped over it from the force of Mike's punch. Mike followed, reaching down and lifting him up by his shirt collar as though he weighed nothing at all. In front of his face, Mike gritted his teeth and gave him a shake. The man's eyes bulged. "Apologize. Now. Or the only thing you'll be eating tonight is your teeth."

A thin line of blood trickled from the man's mouth where Mike's punch had split his lip open. "Sorry," he offered weakly.

Mike gave him a shake. "Not good enough. Not nearly."

"I beg your pardon, ma'am. No insult intended."

Mike put him down, curved his lips up in a cold smile. "Better. Now I suggest you collect your friends and find somewhere else to buy your beer. Red Deer's a few miles that way." He thumbed towards the door.

The three men with him didn't look like they took too kindly to that suggestion. Red Deer was more than a few miles down the road. But a quick survey of the room showed several locals standing at the ready. Vastly outnumbered, they thought better of it and cleared out.

Mike went back to his stool where Grace was waiting. Conversations struck up again.

"You need ice for that hand?" She asked it quietly.

"I'm good." He flexed his knuckles, wincing. Ice would have come in handy but there was no way he'd admit to wanting it.

"Okay then." She started to walk away.

Mike called after her. "You're welcome."

She came back then, and she didn't look happy, speaking in an undertone. "We'll discuss it later."

"Fine. You finish your shift and I'm taking you home."

"Don't you ever get tired of bossing people around?"He chuckled. "I don't boss people around."

"Well, just me then."

"Something like that."

Grace made a frustrated sound in her throat. The man was so exasperating! He wasn't even flustered about causing a bar fight. When this got out...

"Fine." She slammed a glass down on the bar and glared.

Who did he think he was anyway? He waltzed in here on a Friday night acting like he owned the place. Acting like he owned her. There was nothing disgraceful about making an honest living and paying her own way. Even if it meant she had to handle obnoxious men with a little liquor in their system. She wasn't helpless. She knew how to handle herself...either by joking around or ignoring them altogether. And it wasn't like she didn't have other guys around if things got rowdy. It *was* a small town after all. But he just had to take it upon himself to cause a huge scene. To look after everything. He'd been doing that far too much lately. She'd thought the other day they'd finally got past it. They seemed to be friends again, equals. They'd met in the middle the day he'd kissed her. She'd told him it could go nowhere. But nothing she said seemed to get through his thick head.

He'd picked that man up as if he'd weighed nothing at all. He'd done it to defend her honor. She was spitting mad...and even angrier at herself because despite it all, the very memory of it excited her.

As things started to wind down, she escaped to the kitchen for a few minutes. Jack was starting to shut down the kitchen and worked silently as she loaded the dishwasher. She and Mike had never been closer, despite all the arguments. She'd sensed apology in his eyes just before he'd thrown his punch, almost as if to say, *Sorry honey, but I can't let that one slide.* He'd kissed her—not a brotherly kiss, but an all-consuming toe-curling kiss. When they'd done that at his house, she finally understood that he didn't look at her in a brotherly way. He saw her as a woman. As *his* woman. And he'd apologized of all things. Mike never said he was sorry to *anyone.*

She wanted to trust him again. But trusting her heart to someone else came hard.

Nothing was making sense anymore. The closer they got to each other, the more muddled things became. She shouldn't have started any of this. If she could take back that single dance at the Rileys', she thought maybe she would. That had started everything, and now she was going to have to put on the brakes.

Tears stung the backs of her eyes as she placed plates in neat rows on the bottom rack of the dishwasher. All that she wanted was within her reach. And to be fair to him, she was going to have to stop it now, before someone really got hurt. Before she really got hurt.

He was waiting for her when she came out again, his hat still sitting low across his forehead.

"You ready? I'll walk you home."

She should resist, tell him she'd go alone. But he'd only insist anyway. If she were going to set things straight and they were to be just friends after tonight, then she was going to enjoy one last walk home with him.

"I'm ready."

The air outside was fresh and crisp, a respite from the stale air inside the bar. "Frost tonight," she commented as they headed down Main Avenue.

"Feels like it."

Her stomach curled into itself when he took her palm in his and they walked hand in hand. It was a simple gesture, but one so unlike the Mike she knew, her heart wept for what she knew she must do. Things couldn't go any further. She had to pass on any chance with him.

Their steps slowed, lingering, as their breath made white puffs in the air before them. It seemed only seconds and they were before her bungalow. Too short. She wanted all the time she could have with him before sending him away.

"Here we are."

"Thanks for walking me home."

They wandered in as far as her back steps. She was two steps up when she turned. Mike removed his hat, holding it in his right hand as he gazed up at her.

"Can I come in?"

"I don't think so."

He paused, then followed her up the steps. She backed up until she was pressed against the door.

"Then I'll have to kiss you goodnight at the door."

Her body shook, and it wasn't because of the chill. His hips pressed against hers, pinning her in place.

"Don't..."

She may as well have spoken to the air. He was already there, his body covering hers, warm and firm. His hat dropped to the doormat, and he took her mouth completely.

One kiss, just one. Grace sighed into his mouth. The girls had been right. That night when they'd speculated about him. General consensus was that Mike would be a fantastic lover. If he did that as well as he kissed, Grace knew she'd be a very satisfied woman. And as he pulled her against him, she was tempted to find out this once.

Except he'd be disappointed. The thought cooled her considerably. He thought she was something she wasn't...and now that he was obviously looking to start his own family...no, she couldn't face that. This time it would be her doing the leaving, and she regretted it deeply.

She broke the kiss and stepped away, digging into her pockets for her keys.

"Goodnight, Mike."

He put his hand on her screen door, preventing her from opening it. "That's it? After a kiss like that? Do I get to at least know why?"

Perhaps she should just come out with it and reveal all. A great uncomfortable silence would ensue, and she wouldn't have to worry about Mike coming back. He'd be gone for good. Just like Steve, her ex-husband.

But she'd never told a living soul about the consequences of her accident. She wasn't ready. She didn't know if she'd ever be ready.

"I'm sorry. I'm tired. It was a long night."

He seemed to accept her excuse. "And I'm sorry about those idiots. Does that happen a lot?"

"Enough. I could have handled it."

He let go of the door. "Of course you could. You're doing such a bang-up job of handling your life so far."

He was baiting her and she knew it, but it gave her the opportunity she needed to push him away. "Considering it's my life to handle, I don't know why you keep pressing the issue, and why I must keep repeating myself. Your help was not required this evening."

"You're mad I hit him." He stated the obvious, his chin flattening with displeasure.

Heat expanded her chest. Never in her life had a man stood up for her that way, and even as she criticized him for it she knew it was one of those moments she'd cherish forever. For all his faults, Mike knew how to treat a woman. No man would insult her honor when he was around. After years of only having herself to rely on, it was a heady feeling, knowing he was there for her. She wished, somehow, she could be there for him the same way. But Mike never seemed to need anything.

"You would have had the backing of every man there, Mike. They all know you. The tavern's full of locals. If you'd asked those men to leave, they would have."

"And let him call you the equivalent of a tramp? I don't think so."

"He was being a jerk! It doesn't mean you have to turn into one!"

"Now *I'm* a jerk? Wow. So much for a little gratitude!"

"No one invited you to come in tonight, and no one asked for your assistance," she retorted coldly, wrapping her arms around her waist.

"Yeah, because you didn't even bother to tell me this was how you were paying for the new transmission. I had to hear from Alex!"

And Alex had seen fit to tell all and try her hand at matchmaking. It was all starting to make sense now. She uncrossed her arms and took a step, going toe to toe with him.

"And you came in and started a spitting match because someone had a bigger belt buckle than you!"

His gray eyes burned into hers in the dark. "You have to know why I did it."

"It doesn't matter." She swallowed. *Please don't say any more,* she silently begged.

His voice was a husky whisper as he came even closer, their bodies only a shiver away. "I think it does matter. You have to know my feelings for you. Grace, I..."

"Stop, Mike, please." The words came out thick with pent up emotion. "Don't say any more. We can only be friends. Like we used to be."

"I don't believe you. I know how you feel in my arms, how you kiss me...not like old friends. You have to see I've started to settle down. I'm not on the road anymore. I have a business, and a house. Grace, I haven't been able to stop thinking about you since the night we danced. I want a second chance. To do it right this time."

That dance was going to haunt her for the rest of her life, she was sure of it. She should have kept her mouth shut instead of taking the dare. But she couldn't forget the memory of how it felt to be in his arms at last, the smell of him, the way their feet shuffled across the floor as he smiled his crooked, enigmatic smile down at her.

"That night was a mistake on my part." She wanted to get away, he was so close, but there was nowhere to go. Oh Lord, he was trying to make her see that he was worthy of her, and it was breaking her heart. She wanted to be able to offer him what he was asking, but it was impossible. He deserved a woman who could give him what he wanted. A family of his own. One he'd never had before. And she couldn't do that. He said he wouldn't leave her, but she knew deep down that was exactly what would happen in the end.

"I had too much to drink and flirted where I had no right to flirt." She cleared her throat and strengthened her tone. "I'm sorry for giving you the impression there was more there. That's my fault. I did it on a dare."

His face hardened and she felt him close himself off to her. Grace fought back the horrible urge to cry. *Just go,* she pleaded in her head. If he'd leave, she could at least go inside and cry in private.

"I see. Then I guess I'll leave you here."

"I guess so." She knew she shouldn't ask anything of him now, but she couldn't resist. She didn't want to lose his friendship altogether. "Will you do me a favor?"

He picked up his hat and placed it on his head so she couldn't see his eyes. He was shutting her out, just like she wanted. She already missed him.

"Depends."

"Will you tell Johanna to let me know if anything happens with Alex? She's getting closer to her due date, and I'm still worried about her. Let her know if there's anything I can do..."

"I'll tell her."

He didn't say anything more but went down the steps and up the driveway. Grace fumbled with her keys, going into the house and straight through to the front verandah. She watched him walk down the street until he was out of sight.

Then she gave in and let the tears come—hot, stinging ones full of regret for what might have been and what could never be.

· · · · ● ● ● ● · · ·

Grace pocketed her tips and laid her folded apron on top of the bar. Three weeks had passed in a blur. Between her hourly wage and her tips, she'd paid for nearly two-thirds of the repairs on her car. The rest she'd make up with the extra she was making doing books for Circle M. She was tired and happy to be finished, and grateful for the brief, but profitable opportunity.

Keeping busy had kept her mind off Mike too, she thought as she walked home in the early evening dusk. Mike had taken a risk and shown his feelings and she'd done nothing but shut him down. Knowing him as she did, she knew it had to have been a hard thing for him to do. He deserved so much more. For Mike to ask for love... well, it was unheard of. She couldn't return it, no matter how much she wanted to. She'd told him it was a dare, flirting with him. It wasn't strictly true, but it had gotten the job done.

She reached home and entered, turning on lights as she went through. She sighed, grabbing a can of pop from the fridge and going out to her verandah to enjoy the quiet. Mike hadn't noticed her as a girl much, but he'd been a friend despite their age difference back then. If he thought someone was picking on her, he took care of it. When she got her driver's license, he and Connor had taken her out and taught her how to drive a stick shift in Connor's beat-up pickup. After she'd broken up with her high-school boyfriend, he'd found her at her favorite spot, up on top of a hill west of town, looking over the Rockies. She'd been crying, but he'd admitted he'd come there too, to think. Sitting in the tall grass, chewing on hay, they'd talked a lot, and it was there that he'd first leaned over and kissed her. She could still feel the wonder of that moment. For a few short weeks, they had grown closer. He was twenty-one, but their relationship had been tenuous and sweet. They'd held hands. Kissed. Had gone to a movie with Connor and his girlfriend at the time.

Their last date, Grace had made a picnic and they'd gone back to Andersen's field. A few days later she heard from Connor that he was gone.

Andersen's field was still her go-to spot when life got to be too much to handle. But they'd never met there again.

He'd been gone a lot, working, traveling to rodeos. She finished her senior year of high school and went to community college in Red Deer. Her first year she'd met Steve, her software applications instructor, and no one had been there to warn her of moving too fast. She'd married that summer, Steve got a new job in Edmonton, and she went with him without finishing her certificate.

Grace put down the pop can as her stomach churned. She tried not to think about her failed marriage, but sometimes it was hard not to when she was alone on a Saturday night with only the hum of the refrigerator keeping her company. She'd rushed into it, partly out of hurt and partly out of defiance. And what a colossal mistake.

She stared out the window as full dark overcame the sky. It had been a night similar to this, and she'd been driving to the campus to surprise her husband. She hadn't seen the deer by the side of the road, and when it leaped in front of her, she'd hit the brakes and wrenched the wheel.

That was all she remembered. When she woke up, she was in the hospital.

Consistent knocking on her back door brought her to her senses. She shook her head and hurried to see what the matter was. When she turned on the outside light, Mike was standing beneath it.

"What's wrong?" She opened the door without pausing, forgetting all about her earlier mental meanderings. She could tell by the worried lines on his face that something had happened. He hadn't even changed out of his work clothes, despite the hour, and his ever-present hat was missing.

"Connor took Alex to the hospital."

"But her due date is in a few days. There's no cause for worry."

Mike lifted his eyes to hers, and she clearly saw pain there. "She's bleeding. He didn't wait for the ambulance, just put her in the truck and went."

"Oh, God. Come in."

"I'm following him in. If anything happens to her...I don't want him to be alone. She's his entire world."

Grace's lip quivered. Sometimes Mike was so guarded she forgot he had a sensitive heart. Every woman wanted to be loved the way Connor so obviously loved his wife. And of course Mike wanted to be there for his best friend. All their issues were forgotten as she looked into his worried eyes. "I'll go with you."

"I was hoping you'd say that." His cheeks sagged with relief.

She hurried to get her purse, fighting against the sense of doom that tingled down her spine.

When she came back, Mike was waiting, holding the door for her. "Thank you for coming, Grace," he murmured as she locked the door.

"I didn't want to do this alone."

She was touched that finally she could do something for him, after all the times he'd looked out for her. Any anger she'd felt about him being too protective evaporated when she saw the concern on his face. He was the same way with all the people that meant so much to him. "I wouldn't have it any other way," she replied, opening the door to his truck and climbing into the passenger side. "Alex and Connor are... well, we've all been linked for a long time, Mike."

Mike spun out the drive and headed towards Main Avenue and the road east out of town. "Connor's the closest thing to a brother I've ever had, and Alex has made me a part of their family. If anything happens to her or the baby..."

Grace reached over and put a hand on his arm. "Don't think like that. Look at all they've been through already. She's tough and strong willed. We're all going to come through this..."

Her voice trailed off. It was so hard to focus on Alex right now when the very situation brought everything back to her so vividly. She looked over at Mike's tight profile. He was so worried over Alex and the baby. And all she could offer him was friendship. She missed the easy way they used to have with each other before she'd complicated things, and more than ever she was convinced that they couldn't be both friends *and* lovers. If nothing else, she'd sit with him tonight in his worry. She'd be there for him in the only way she could.

It seemed to take forever to finally reach the hospital. Together they strode through the emergency doors to the triage desk. The nurse there said that Alex had already been taken to obstetrics and gave them directions.

The waiting room in labor and delivery was strangely empty and a television played to a non-existent audience. Magazines were scattered on a table and a vending machine stood in a corner. Grace dug in her wallet for coins.

"Mike, I'm going to ask about Alex. Will you get us some coffee?" She pressed the change into his hand, hoping giving him something to do would help.

He nodded.

When she came back, he was sitting on the loveseat, holding both cups and staring at the television screen without seeing anything. It was tuned to the news, the anchor woman's muffled voice providing the only sound in the room.

"All they'd tell me is that the doctors are in with her. But I asked her to let Connor know we're here if she sees him."

They waited in silence. There was nothing to say.

Grace wondered if Steve had waited this way while waiting for word about her. Even now, the antiseptic smell, the hushed tones, brought back memories she'd rather forget. By the time she'd awakened it was all over, and all that was left to do was heal, or at least try to. And Steve would never speak of the accident afterwards. Once, during an argument, she'd pried it out of him that he'd seen her with tubes and wires coming out of everywhere and that from his perspective, she hadn't been the wife he knew when she'd been like that. For a long time, she'd wondered how to make him see she was still his wife, and not the prone patient hooked up to machines. She'd tried right up until the end.

She was surprised to find tears in her eyes. She'd cried about that night, her failed marriage, lots in the beginning, but it was all in the past now. Had been since she moved back only a little more than two years after leaving in the first place. As far as the town knew, her marriage hadn't worked out, plain and simple. Some said she married too young. She knew the truth. She hadn't stepped foot in a hospital since. Not until right now, and being here now left her raw and aching.

Mike's hand slid over and covered hers. "You okay?"

"I'm all right." She carefully kept her gaze away from his. He had an uncanny ability to see too much. "Wish we'd hear something."

Connor came around the corner, wearing a disposable gown and stripping off latex gloves. "The nurse said you were here."

Mike and Grace stood together. "And?"

Connor made it brief. "She's getting an epidural right now. Then I'm going into the O.R. with her. This baby's coming by C-section."

"Alex is okay?"

The night seemed to have put ten years on Connor's face. "She's hanging in there, but she's weak and they said the baby's in distress." His voice broke a little and he cleared his throat. "She's a trooper. Refuses to go under, insists on being awake for the whole thing. I've got to get back. But I'm glad you came. I'll let you know as soon as I have news."

"Connor?"

Grace's voice interrupted his departure and he turned back.

"Give Alex our love and let her know we're waiting to meet the newest Madsen."

"I will."

He strode back down the hall.

"I hate waiting."

Mike's responding laugh was a dry huff. "I don't think anyone really enjoys it." They walked back over to the love seat, consumed with worry for Alex and the baby, needing a distraction.

"If you could be doing anything right now, what would it be?"

He sat down. "Come here, and I'll show you." He patted the cushion beside him.

When she sat, he put his arm along the top of the back and curved it around her, pulling her close. She shifted, angling herself slightly sideways and leaning into his body, pulling his arm around her securely. Even knowing it was wrong, nothing felt better than being held in his arms.

"Connor's worried." His voice rumbled softly against her hair.

"Of course he is."

"They lost one already, you know?"

She cranked her head to the side, trying to look up at him. "They did?"

"She had a miscarriage before this pregnancy. Connor told me when she went into early labor the first time."

"I didn't know that." Now all the caution and worry made sense.

"Right now, Alex is in there fighting for their baby."

Her throat closed against the ball of emotion that settled there.

"Right now, Grace, holding you is the only thing that makes sense."

Grace gave up fighting him. Nothing else mattered than the right outcome for the people that had come to mean so much to them both. She wrapped her arms around his strong one, turning her head into his shoulder and dropping a kiss against the muscle there.

"Then hold on to me, Mike."

CHAPTER 7

Connor didn't return with the news, but a nurse on silent shoes did, at two in the morning.

"Mr. Gardner?"

Mike shook Grace gently, never taking his eyes off the sight of her sleeping. Strands of her pale hair fell over her cheek, lending a look of innocence. Her face was peaceful, even more beautiful than usual with the lines of stress gone.

"Grace, wake up."

She sighed and he felt her burrow deeper into his arms. It was so right, having her there. At times he was sure she felt it, too. When she stopped fighting him, the connection between them was undeniable. Strong and pure.

But there was news and as much as he wished he could hold her all night, he reluctantly said her name again.

"Grace."

Her eyelids fluttered open, staring up into his and his breath caught. Her lips were slightly open, and her gaze was as blue as a September sky. In that one unguarded moment, he knew she'd lied about the only friends part. Something was holding her back, but he knew there was more when she looked at him that way. They had a connection. She was as tangled up in him as he was in her.

"The nurse is here."

She sat up, fully awake now, and Mike immediately missed the feeling of her warm body curled against his. Grace tucked the errant strands of hair behind her ears and straightened her clothing, looking up at the nurse.

"Alex? And the baby?"

The nurse smiled. "Both fine. Mr. and Mrs. Madsen are resting, and the baby is a strapping boy. Mr. Madsen asked me to tell you that his name is James Michael Madsen."

Mike grinned, a flash of brightness that sucked the stress out of the room and filled it with brilliance. "Son of a gun."

"He also sent this message." She pulled out a small piece of paper. "Tell Grace to get Mike home and make him sleep, because I'm taking a few days off."

Grace laughed. "If they're resting, we'll just go. We can come back another time and see them. Thank you for letting us know."

"You're entirely welcome." With a parting smile, she was gone again on quiet shoes.

Now that the heavy feeling was gone, Mike's grin was wide and relaxed. "James Michael. I can't believe he did that. I had a feeling he'd name it after Jim if it was a boy, but not me."

He leaned back in his chair, remembering the day Connor's family had died and the guilt that Connor had carried around for years. "I was with him when he got the news, you know," he told Grace softly, like if saying it louder would be disrespectful. "A bunch of us had gone to Sylvan Lake for the day. We swam, took out a boat, had a cooler of beer...just the guys out for a day of R and R."

Grace was turned and watching him now. "I didn't know that."

"I'll never forget the look on his face as long as I live," Mike continued. "He insisted on driving down to the accident scene alone. And he's never talked about it since. I know I'm not Jim, but he's the closest thing to a brother I've ever had."

The very idea that someone thought enough of him to bestow any part of his name on their child just seemed too huge to comprehend.

Grace smiled up at him. "You're touched."

"Of course I am." He looked down at her, confused at her obvious surprise, still reeling from the news and the feel of her body against his.

"You don't think you're special enough for someone to name a kid after you?"

"Something like that."

"Don't underestimate yourself, Mike. You've got a family already, whether you like it or not. Just because they're not blood, doesn't matter."

He gripped her fingers in his. "I'm beginning to see that."

He let his eyes fall warmly on hers. For a moment he considered kissing her as their gazes clung, but then he straightened as if nothing had passed between them. It wasn't the time. But he wanted to come up with some way to keep her with him longer. If he kept trying, perhaps he could break down the barriers she kept erecting between them.

"I'm not going to be able to sleep now. How about I buy you breakfast?"

"At two-thirty in the morning?"

"Why not? There's got to be something open twenty-four hours."

"I don't know, I..."

He tugged on her hand, leading her to the elevators. "There's blueberry pancakes in it for you."

"Now you're playing dirty. You *know* those are my favorite."

When she pulled back on his hand he paused. Of course, just because he was pumped didn't mean she was. He'd almost forgotten how hard she'd been working. She'd want to get home and rest. She probably had a busy day tomorrow.

"I didn't think," he apologized, slowing down and pressing the down button on the elevator. "You must be tired. And with your schedule..."

"I do have a demanding boss."

He wrinkled his brow. "Someone giving you a hard time?"

"He's expecting me to show up in the morning and if I stay out all night with you, I'm not going to be much good."

"He won't understand about Alex? Which job are we talking about here?" If it came to it, he'd explain to this person himself. He stood taller, squaring his shoulders.

"I guess I could talk to him." Her eyes twinkled up at him.

Mike stared down at her as a pretty smile curved across her face.

"So, how about it boss? You gonna be mad if I don't show up in the morning?"

He grinned, realizing she was teasing him, and he teased back. "I can guarantee that all it'll cost you is a bite of pancake and a smile."

"Then let's go. I don't think I could sleep now, either."

· · • • · • • · · ·

Mike killed the engine and Grace pressed a hand to her belly.

Her house waited, dark and lonely, and she didn't want to go inside. She was still too fragile. At the hospital she'd fallen asleep, but even in her slumber she could hear the beep of machines and hushed voices. When Mike had awakened her, she'd been so glad to see his face above hers. She felt safe there. For a moment, as she'd looked into his eyes, there'd been nothing but the two of them in the universe. And then she'd awakened fully, getting the good news about Alex and the baby.

On the heels of that was a keen sadness of knowing what had brought her to this point in her life. She'd painted on a smile, happy for the good news and pleased for Mike. She'd teased Mike, thinking that diversion was as good a plan as any. But even breakfast at the twenty-four-hour restaurant hadn't helped. She'd thought by staying away, giving herself some time to acclimatize, she'd be fine, but exactly the opposite had happened. It had given her feelings time to build until they were nearly overwhelming. She was a mess.

"Well, we're here." Mike's voice interrupted her thoughts and she jumped. "Hey, are you okay?" He shifted in the seat, looking over at her. "You're white as a sheet."

"I'm just tired," she managed to get out. It was a lie.

Over pancakes and coffee, she'd fought the feeling that she was losing complete control of her life. She'd tried to enjoy Mike's company, share in his joy about baby James. But seeing him that way was a stark reminder of all he wanted now and all she couldn't give him. Of all that she wanted to give him, even knowing there was no possible way she could. And the heartbreak of losing chance after chance.

Every day for six years she'd thought she'd dealt with the changes fate had brought to her life, but now she knew she really hadn't succeeded. Being in the hospital had been difficult and had brought back memories of the last time she'd been there. But she and Mike had been focused on Alex and the baby and somehow even that had delayed her reaction. But now, knowing everyone was safe and happy and healthy, it drained every bit of strength from her. If she went inside now, alone, she wasn't sure she could make it through five minutes without completely losing it. And that thought scared the hell out of her. She knew how long it had taken her to function again after the last meltdown. She'd spent several months numb to everything, protecting herself in a shell of not feeling anything at all. She'd do anything to keep that from happening again.

"You want to come in?"

"You need your sleep. I've kept you out late enough, don't you think?"

She regarded him in the dim glow of the dash lights. He was so strong, so sure of himself. All legs and boots and lean muscle, always ready to do what needed to be done. A man to count on. Could she count on him now?

"I..." She swallowed. "I don't want to be alone."

"You want me to sit with you?"

Her breaths came shallow and quick. "I want..." She looked into his eyes. His were earnest and open, inviting her to explain. He waited patiently, one wrist slung over the steering wheel.

She wanted to be with him, and it frightened her to admit it out loud. She glanced back at the house. The other alternative was to go in there alone and finally face the fact that she could never be what she wanted to be. Dealing with that right now was far scarier than facing this attraction, or whatever it was they'd been doing lately. Once he knew the truth, he'd run for sure. What if this was her only chance? Could she let it get away? Let him get away?

Taking a breath, she blurted it out. "I want to be with you, Mike."

"Be with me," he echoed. He didn't sound sure of what that meant, and his eyebrows furrowed in the middle.

She faced him squarely. Yes, being with Mike was what she wanted, so much more than facing what was waiting for her inside. For a second, images flashed through her head like the rapid shutter of a camera: the red lights of the ambulance, the drip of her IV, the sound of the doctor's voice and the kind look in his eyes, Steve's telling her he was leaving, Connor's face tonight. She couldn't breathe, couldn't feel. And she needed to feel right now, something other than pain and failure. She needed life and hope.

He was waiting.

"I want you." She said the words with her heart in her throat and saw his eyes widen. "I've always wanted you, Mike."

"Grace, I..." He paused. Then blindly reached for the keys and shut off the engine, leaving the truck still and silent.

"Maybe we should talk about this."

Grace's responding laugh was dry and humorless. The very idea of the reticent Mike wanting to "talk" about things was out of character. He was putting her off; she could feel it. Humiliation stung at the back of her eyelids, and she grabbed her purse with one hand while struggling to open her door with the other. "Never mind," she stammered, fighting with the strap of her purse which got entangled on the seatbelt. "Forget I mentioned it."

She ripped the strap free and slammed the door, trotting to the house before she lost it completely.

His door slammed and he called her name.

Her keys were buried in her purse and she ripped open the zipper, frantically searching. What had she been thinking, propositioning him? This time she didn't have alcohol as an excuse.

"Wait."

He put his hand around her wrist and her fingers stilled.

"Grace, don't run away from me. You've been running all fall. I can feel it. Even though we were getting closer, you kept holding something back. I just want to know why that changed tonight."

She turned slowly. His gray eyes were asking hers for an honest answer. The yellow glow from her porch light danced off the copper tints of his hair. Maybe this would be her only chance, and if that were the case, did she really want to spoil it by admitting to him she could never give him the family, the kind of home life he wanted? Wouldn't it be better to go away with one beautiful memory of what loving him was like? It certainly beat the alternative of sending him away and having to face all her shortcomings alone as the sun came up.

"I've wanted you for nearly half my life. Tonight I realized I was tired of fighting it. Of thinking too much, doubting every move. Of doubting you. I want to feel. And I want it to be with you. Is that wrong?"

"No, baby, it's not wrong." His voice was husky with relief, and he pulled her close, tucking her within his arms.

She felt his lips press against her hair. One large, gentle hand slid up her back and beneath her hair, taking command of her neck.

"I want you too, Grace. I've thought about it ever since the night we danced. Since long before then."

"You have?"

He tipped her neck up. "You don't believe me?"

Her breath came quicker at his burning gaze. "It's hard to believe."

He didn't answer. Instead he bent his head and kissed her, taking her mouth completely. His lips commanded hers to open and his arms pulled her close against his body.

He pressed his forehead to hers as the kiss broke off. "Do you believe me now?"

Grace slid her hand up his arm, marveling at the feel of the muscles corded beneath his shirt. "But you never said anything before."

"I was waiting for you to be ready. Hell, I was waiting for me to be ready. It took a long time for me to get to a place where I was ready to stop running. Even after I moved back for good...I didn't think you'd give me a second glance. I left you before...I didn't want to be unfair to you." He paused, then commanded, "Look at me."

She did, captured by the honesty in his eyes.

"I'm not running now, Grace."

She lifted his hand and pressed a kiss to the palm. Releasing it, she reached into her purse and got out her house keys. With shaking hands, she fed the key into the lock and opened the door.

She left the foyer light off, instead walking straight through to the kitchen. The outside door shut with a click, and she heard Mike turning the lock again. The simple sound was filled with such intimacy—the closing out of another world, keeping them in their own cocoon of each other.

She stood in the middle of the kitchen floor, suddenly unsure of what to do. It seemed everything was firsts today. First visit to the hospital since the accident. The first time with Mike. The first time she was going to have sex since her divorce. She shuddered as his hands fell on to her shoulders and his body warmed the skin of her back through her sweater. Her eyes slid closed, her body heavy with languor. Six long years. It seemed an eternity since she'd been twenty-one.

"I'm not sure what to do," she whispered softly.

He chuckled, the vibration of his chest causing rippling reactions through her stomach. "You *were* married, Grace. It's like riding a bike."

"Yes, but..." Her voice dropped off. This was weird. This was the problem with falling for someone who was also your friend, she realized. She wanted him to see her as brand new, as his lover, yet at the same time longed to reveal things to him, things that were safe because of their friendship. For a moment she wanted to believe that he meant what he said. That he wouldn't leave her.

"But?" He turned her to face him. "You keep looking away from me. Are you scared?"

"Not of you," she admitted. Still she couldn't look in his eyes.

He bent at the knees so their eyes were level. "Are you telling me this is your first time since your divorce?"

She turned her head away, but not before she felt heat creep up her cheeks. "You must think I'm...oh, I'm not sure what you think."

"I'll tell you what I think." His hands skimmed down her ribs and settled at her waist. "I think I'm glad. I find I'm very relieved that there hasn't been anyone since."

"Why?" His thumbs toyed with the waist of her jeans, and she couldn't help but meet his eyes, colorlessly dark in the dim light.

"Because I hate the thought of any man's hands on you but mine."

Her breath caught as his fingers played with the hem of her sweater. His lips touched the side of her ear, down the lobe. "Right now, I'd kill any man who dared to lay a hand on you."

For weeks she'd fought his possessiveness, but now, in his arms, she reveled in it. Gloried in it. Right now, in this moment, she was his. There was nothing she'd ever wanted more.

Her fingers trembling with anticipation, she undid the bottom button of his shirt, then the next, and the next, until finally the cotton gaped open, revealing a slice of strong chest. He cupped her jaws with his hands and pulled her against him, dropping his mouth to hers. The man knew how to kiss. She moaned deep in her throat and his arms tightened around her, so close now that her back arched a little. Her hand slipped beneath his shirt, touching the warm skin along his ribs. The tips of her fingers traced a scar, the skin smoother and tighter along the line of the wound. He lifted his mouth long enough to say against her lips, "When I was eighteen and still green."

She'd be lying if she said his rough rodeo past didn't add a little excitement to the puzzle that was Mike. But now she knew that this side, the side that he was giving to her, was more than she'd ever imagined she'd have. It was strong and beautiful, and she wished he would look at her forever the way he was looking at her now.

She reached for the hem of her sweater and pulled it over her head, standing before him now in only her low-slung jeans and plain black bra.

Without saying one more word, she took him by the hand and led him to the bedroom.

CHAPTER 8

Grace rolled over at the sound of raindrops hitting the glass of her bedroom window. She looked at her clock radio: one forty-two. She'd slept through the morning. A deep, dark, satisfied sleep.

She rose, grabbing her robe from behind the door and shoving her arms through the sleeves. Memories of what had happened in the early hours still caused tingles to spiral through her body. Now things were even more complicated, if that were possible. Just when she decided that she and Mike had to remain friends, she'd done something so insane she needed her head examined. Sleeping with him was avoidance of her own hurts, pure and simple, and worse, he'd started showing her a new side of him. One that made him even more irresistible. Now she knew he was tender, caring and completely consuming as a lover. More than she'd ever imagined in her dreams. It wasn't supposed to happen like this!

She wandered to the kitchen, thinking a cup of tea might soothe her. She'd make some toast and have a think about what to do next.

Entering the kitchen she saw the folded paper on top of the kitchen table, propped up against one of the pewter candlesticks. She opened it and saw his scrawl, legible only because she was so familiar with it. *Hope you slept well. I'll pick you up at five thirty so we can visit Alex and the baby. Love, M.*

Love, M? Grace stared at the writing, her heart sinking. Oh, what had she done? She should have known Mike wasn't a typical guy. He was the kind of guy who never wrote notes or said the word *love* unless he absolutely had to. He was a man who'd grown up with little affection in his life. One who took every bit of it to heart but rarely gave it out. He thought she didn't understand, but she did. And he was suddenly turning the tables and giving it to her. A woman who desperately wanted it but didn't deserve it. Didn't know what to do with it.

At some point he'd awakened and left. That didn't hurt her feelings; she knew he had a ranch to run, especially in Connor's absence.

What frightened her to death was what in the world she'd say to him when she saw him again.

Schoolgirl fantasies were gone. She was crazy about him. Had fought it, told herself she was wrong for him, picked arguments against their developing intimacy. But she'd awakened in the solitude of her room, with the warm feel of him still in the sheets. She admitted to herself that it had always been Mike for her, even after he'd abandoned her. Her feelings for him had dictated so many choices in her life, good and bad. They would be the albatross around her neck for as long as she lived.

Now she had actually taken advantage of him. Used his feelings to her own purpose and she was deeply sorry for it. Sorry that she hadn't been able to be completely honest with him because she was terrified of losing her one chance to know what it was like to be loved by him.

Somehow, she had to get through the visit to the hospital. Then she was going to have to talk to Mike. She had to tell him the truth. It was the only thing that was fair.

· · • •• • • • · ·

Mike picked her up at five thirty as promised. He ran a hand through his hair before opening the door to his truck, expecting to do the proper thing and go in to get her, usher her to the truck and out of the light rain. But before he could do it, she met him coming around the front of the truck instead of giving him time to come in, the hood of her raincoat protecting her hair and making her blue eyes stand out like beacons.

"Hey," he offered as a greeting and accompanying it with a smile.

She was so beautiful, he realized, even more so after what had transpired last night. Now he knew the sweet taste of her; the feel of her soft skin beneath his fingertips. The way she arched her neck and whispered his name in the shadows of dawn. Now he knew what it was like to be hers, and he knew more than ever that he wanted to be with her for more than just a single night. He imagined her in his bed at the new house; drinking coffee with him at the kitchen table in the dew-kissed mornings. He wanted to make up for the past. Show her she could trust him to stay.

He leaned in and dropped a light kiss on her surprised lips, the strawberry taste of her gloss clinging to his mouth. He pulled away, smiling down into her eyes before going to open her door. Silently she climbed up into the cab, settling herself while he slammed the door behind her.

"You're quiet." He put the truck in reverse and slung his arm over the back of the seat, negotiating his way out on to the street.

"Just tired."

He was charmed to see a blush infuse her cheeks. He didn't need to say anything. They both knew the sun had already been up by the time they'd fallen asleep, and it had changed to rain by the time he'd awakened. She'd been naked and in his arms, and when he quietly left, she was still curled up in the bedding, warm and well loved. If he could, he'd forget all about the hospital and go back there again. But Connor was expecting them, and he had no idea how to suggest such a thing to Grace.

He turned his attention to driving, gesturing with a thumb toward a plastic container on her lap. "What's in there?"

"Cookies. Chocolate chocolate chip."

"Chocolate overload?"

"Alex's favorite, I've learned. She's going to be in there a few days and eating hospital food." Grace grimaced with disgust. "She can do with some treats, trust me."

The change of subject relaxed the atmosphere in the truck. They let the radio fill the comfortable silence as they drove to the hospital. Once there, they made their way directly to the maternity wing and from there to Alex's room, just down the hall from the nursery. Mike looked in at all the babies lined up in their clear plastic bassinettes but didn't see any with the name Madsen on the card. He wondered how many of these tiny parcels were wanted and loved and how many had been surprises and complications, like he'd been. He watched as one baby—a girl—waved a tiny mittened fist in the air as she cried, and he wondered if anyone had come to see him when he was born. It was a question he didn't dwell on long, for he knew he would never know the answer now.

There was at least one baby in this hospital that he knew had been wanted. Baby James was lucky. He'd been planned and loved long before he'd ever been born. And that was how he wanted it for his own children someday. To shower them with love and to let them know how wanted they had been.

Alex was sitting up in bed, finishing her supper when Mike and Grace walked in. Connor sat in a vinyl chair beside her, and the rolling bassinette was by the window. Mike caught a glimpse of white and blue blanket.

"I see our timing's right. I brought dessert," Grace announced. She held out the container, smiling when Alex beamed up at her. Mike went over to the window next to Connor's chair.

"Connor told me you guys stayed last night. I appreciate it."

"We were worried," Mike chimed in. "But you did great, Alex."

"I did, didn't I? And what do you think of our little Jamie?"

Connor lifted the tiny blue bundle out of the bed, cradling him in his arms. "He's got great lungs already," he joked. "When he's hungry, you know it."

"Like his daddy," Alex added. She shifted tenderly in the bed.

"You must be sore," Grace remarked, but her voice lacked its usual vigor. She went to Alex and helped adjust her pillow. "C-section isn't easy, huh."

Mike tilted his head and watched Grace. Normally she was easy and welcoming, but for some reason she seemed tense and awkward. There seemed to be some strain around her lips, and her eyes seemed to evade rather than invite.

"I thought labor with Maren was bad, but right now I'm just so drained, you know?"

Grace stepped back but Alex reached out for her hand. "But that doesn't mean I'm not glad to see you. I am. Profoundly. Especially if that's chocolate in that dish."

"Would I bring you anything else?" She opened the lid on the dish, holding it out for Alex to pick a cookie.

Mike took off his coat and laid it over the back of the second chair. "Hey, you wanna hold him?" Connor's voice came quietly from beside him.

He pushed back his hat a little. Hold the baby? It wasn't something he'd ever done before. He'd played with Maren, but not when she was this young. He'd always let someone else do the holding. But times were changing, by the minute it seemed. He looked over at Grace, perched on the edge of the bed with Alex and chatting over cookies. He could easily picture her with a baby in her arms, one with white-blond hair and big blue eyes. And the thought of Grace having anyone else's babies...

Now that was a picture he couldn't reconcile. No way.

"Go ahead. You'll be fine."

Mike made a vee with his arms and Connor shifted the blue-and-white bundle. "Make sure you support his head and it's all good."

Mike shifted his arm so that the tiny head was cushioned against his bicep. He looked down at the tiny face, the nearly transparent eyelids, and the way Jamie's lips sucked in and out as he slept. Mike crossed one ankle over the other, leaning back against the windowsill and making himself comfortable.

A complete little person. Warm and trusting. And he was surprised to discover that holding him was the most natural thing in the world.

His eyes met Grace's and held, burning with the remembrance of making love only hours before. Her soft sighs in the gray darkness. The silken touch of her skin against his.

"It's about time."

Connor's voice interrupted. Grace ripped her gaze away from Mike's and turned her attention to Connor, confused. "About time?"

"That you two finally came to your senses." He grinned widely at his wife. "You owe me ten bucks. I said it would be before Thanksgiving."

"Sneaky." Alex grumbled at her husband. "That's only a few days away."

Mike's smile only widened. Why shouldn't he be happy? He'd thought about being with Grace for months, and things were finally moving forward with them. Their friendship had deepened. And last night...last night had been indescribable. He felt a connection with her than he'd never felt before.

"I think we're busted, Grace." He adjusted the baby and winked at Alex. "Seems you had it figured out before we did. Better late than never though."

He looked at Grace. She was sitting stiffly on the bed, and the thin smile she pasted on her face wasn't real. Dread curled through his belly. Was she regretting last night, then?

"So, what happened between you two? No sense keeping secrets now."

Mike could clearly see that Grace was uncomfortable and kept to his habit of few words. "I don't know what you're talking about," he answered cryptically.

Alex nudged Grace with a hand. "And look at that. Holding Jamie as if he did it every day."

Grace dutifully looked up at him. And what he saw in her eyes shocked him.

Sadness. Deep-in-the-soul sorrow. And for some reason she looked almost apologetic. Why in the world would there be tears fluttering on her lashes?

Alex didn't even seem to notice how quiet Grace had gotten. Baby James started to fuss, and Mike started moving his arms in a soothing motion, his eyes never leaving Grace's wounded ones.

"Just think, Mike, what kind of babies you two could have."

Babies. His and Grace's. Instantly his face warmed. What if...oh God. They'd been so tired, so keyed up he hadn't even given protection a second thought. What if Grace ended up pregnant after last night? He felt none of the dread he thought he'd expect in such a situation. Instead, the idea of having babies with Grace was distinctly alluring. His gaze darted to her belly and back up.

Apparently she was having the same thought, because all the color had drained from her face. He saw her visibly exhale, and then gasp for air.

Without a word, she jumped off the bed and darted from the room.

"What in the world?" Alex looked to Connor and Mike. "Did I say something?"

"I don't know," Mike answered. He handed Jamie back to Connor. "But I'm going after her."

He jogged out of the room. If she were worried about getting pregnant, he could reassure her on that score. He certainly wouldn't abandon her, if that was her worry. Exactly the opposite. At the end of the hall, he saw the staircase door slide shut. When he got there, she was halfway down the first flight, sitting on the cold metal risers and crying so hard each sob was a gulp for air.

"My God, Grace! What's wrong?"

"Just leave me alone!"

"Not likely. Not when you're like this." He lifted her off the steps and folded her into his arms.

She sagged against him for a few minutes until she regained some sense of control. But when he took her by the shoulders, he felt the tremors there. Her face was pale, her eyes haunted with misery.

"Grace, if this is about us forgetting to use a condom last night..."

"A condom?" The words came out coated with disbelief. "You think..."

"It's my fault, but I just want you to know that if you get pregnant, it'll be okay." He dropped light kisses on her bruised eyelids. "More than okay, in fact. You have to know I wouldn't leave you. Not again. Please believe me."

It seemed to be the exact *wrong* thing to say. Her breath started jerking again, holding in sobs that were fighting to get out.

He cursed, clearly afraid for her now. She was as close to breaking as he'd ever seen her. "We need to get you out of here."

"I want to believe...I can't...I mean we need to...I have to tell you something Mike, and I—" The words just kept stammering out, making no sense.

"Not here."

She nodded, her breath coming in short spurts. "I hate hospitals, did you know that?"

It explained a lot about his sense of something holding her back the last few days. Now that he thought about it, each time they'd come through the hospital doors she'd donned some sort of invisible armor. "I'll go back and get our coats and take you home. We can talk there."

"Thank you."

When he was gone, she sat back down on the steps, trembling. It had been Alex's words that set her off. Between the hospital and the baby and her exploding feelings for Mike, she'd been a bomb ready to go off.

What kind of babies you two could have...could have...could have...

Those words echoed in her head over and over. This was supposed to be a happy day. No beeps or hushed, worried voices. No sickness, just joy at a healthy baby boy being brought into the world. But that wasn't what it meant to her. It meant nothing less than complete devastation and she was strangled by her own despair. Now Mike was worried about not using protection and that she might be pregnant. If it weren't so heartbreaking, the irony would be hilarious.

Mike came back with their things, gently helping her with her coat before donning his own.

"What did they say?"

"They're just worried about you. Alex is sure she said something wrong, but I assured her you'd be fine." He zipped up his jacket.

"Thank you."

"Except you're not fine."

He took her elbow and they went down the rest of the steps to the first floor, then out through the lobby and to the parking lot. Once in the truck, he turned to her. "Where do you want to go?"

She didn't want to go home, that much she knew. She'd hidden away in her house far too much already. Besides, right now home was full of memories of Mike, and she was going to find it difficult enough to get through this without remembering how he'd kissed her in the kitchen or how they'd made love in her bed less than twenty-four hours ago.

"I want to go to the ranch," she said.

It was full dark by the time they got there. The only light on was the living room, where presumably Johanna was watching television. The rain of the day had soaked into the grass, heightening the musty smell of fall leaves. "Do you want to go inside?"

She shook her head. "No. I need to be out here, where I can breathe."

He led her around the house to the pergola that Connor had built. The rose bush that had bloomed around the bottom of it this year was now brown and brittle. Wood and iron benches flanked it, surrounded by small perennial beds—Alex's handiwork.

Grace went over to the latticed arch and ran her fingers down the painted wood.

"Connor built this for Alex, did you know that?"

"He built it for their wedding." Mike's voice was low and strong in the silence of the evening.

Weddings and babies. Things that Grace had always wanted. But she'd lost one and couldn't have the other.

The loss of it overwhelmed her and tears came again. She went over to the bench and sat down, crying quietly, the drops falling hot and painful on her hands.

Without a word, Mike sat beside her, took her in his arms and let her sob it out.

When it seemed that she was quieting, he rubbed her back gently. "You going to tell me what happened in there? What's causing all this pain? Because it's clear to me this has been building up for a long time."

Grace leaned against the hard wall of his chest, too exhausted to move. Right now it felt as though the whole universe was conspiring against her. She'd been the one to start the ball rolling. She'd wanted to be with Mike, but it had never been like this. Fantasizing about him as a lover wasn't remotely the same as falling for him as a man. Now even Alex was pairing her up with Mike, making more out of it than could ever be. Mike himself seemed happy about how things had developed between them.

That in itself was a complete turnaround. For years he'd been Mike Gardner, bronc rider, self-proclaimed bachelor and all-around tough guy. But not now, and not with her. Now he was Mike, businessman, friend, lover, and potential family man. The one person she could count on. And he needed to know she was not who he thought she was. Even if it meant she lost him.

He ran a warm hand over her back. "I'm sorry, Grace. I screwed things up between us and I'm trying to make up for it now."

"What?"

She lifted her head. He thought this was about him. And she supposed in a way it was. When he'd treated her like she was disposable, she'd retaliated by moving away, marrying Steve. It didn't make sense now, but at eighteen it sure had. His leaving had precipitated her making the biggest mistake of her life.

But it was her mistake to own, not his. He was not to blame.

He didn't look away but faced her straight on, the very picture of honesty. "I need to tell you why I disappeared. I need you to understand."

He drew back a little and took her hands in his larger ones. "I'd gone my whole life without love. I knew how to deal with that. But I didn't know how to deal with the feelings I had for you. And suddenly you had feelings for me. Being with you was...beautiful. It was all I had imagined and for that reason I was terrified that it wasn't real, and it wouldn't last.

"I knew I couldn't bear it if you broke up with me. I had come to care for you that much. You have to understand that every time I thought I'd found a family, I'd been shipped off somewhere else. Maggie was the only one who put up with me and I didn't make it easy, even for her."

He sighed. "Don't you get it Grace? I was falling in love with you and too scared to admit it. So I did what was easy. I left."

Oh God, he was laying his heart bare, and she didn't think she could take much more.

"It wasn't easy for me."

"I know. When I came back, you'd married and divorced and were living in your little bungalow. I told myself you'd moved on and that I deserved that. I knew that I had blown my chance with you and that it would be wrong for me to ask for a second one. I didn't want to lose what friendship we had left. But then at the Rileys', you gave me hope. I knew if I just had time, you would..."

"STOP."

Grace lifted her hand, closing her eyes and willing him to stop talking. He couldn't know what his protests of constancy were doing to her.

"You need to stop, Mike. You broke my trust when you walked away. Not only walked away but did it without saying a word. No call, no letter, no nothing. How do I know that you won't leave again when something gets to be too much for you?"

"Because I grew up, Grace. And I learned from my mistake. That's how you know."

"What do you want, Mike? What are your dreams, your hopes? What's your vision of the future?"

She held her breath, fearful of how he'd answer yet needing to know.

He lifted his hand, gently covering her cheek with his palm. "I see you, Grace. I see you and me and Circle M. I see our children. For the first time, I *see* a future."

Tears gathered in her eyes. "And what if one of those things doesn't work out? Will you cut and run if it gets too much?"

His brow furrowed. "I don't understand. What are you asking?"

"I'm sorry," she murmured, grasping the hand on her cheek and drawing it down into her lap. "It must seem like I'm talking in riddles. And I'll explain, but you have to let me, or I won't get through it."

The cool of the evening seeped through her coat and into her bones. This, then, was the moment of truth. This was the test of his devotion and she'd give anything to be able to avoid it. But it had to be done. Sooner rather than later. To let things go on was only asking for greater hurt.

"I just couldn't handle it...the hospital...the baby...the look on your face when you held him..."

His wide hand squeezed her knee. Regret flooded through her. He deserved so much more. He'd done nothing except drive her crazy with his constant meddling—his way of showing his support and caring. He'd made amends for the past. She'd put the wheels of all this in motion and now it was her job to stop it.

She pulled away from his touch and looked up into his face. The moon tried hard to peek through the clouds now that the rain had passed. His eyes were soft with concern for her, a tenderness that broke her heart.

"I should have told you long ago. But...but I've never told anyone what I'm about to tell you. It was just too hard."

"Whatever it is, just tell me." He tried a reassuring smile. "I know you, Grace. It can't possibly be that bad. You're too good a person."

She wasn't, and that was what he didn't understand. He'd somehow put her on a pedestal, thinking she was something she was not, thinking it was his job to protect her. But the damage had already been done.

She leaned back against his arm. "When I left Sundre for school, you were still drifting. I was angry with you for what you had done to me and in a way, I suppose I was determined to show you that someone cared about me the way you didn't. The logic was flawed but I was thinking with my feelings. I was only eighteen. I met Steve and everything happened very quickly. By the time you were back working in town, we were married and moving to Edmonton. And you were gone again. When I came back a few years later, you were still gone. Riding the circuit. Working at ranches. Whatever suited you at the time. You were always...temporary. And I kept to myself, telling myself that I wanted to preserve the friendship we'd had before. Mom and Dad had retired and gone to Edson. But I didn't know where else to go but home."

Mike's hand stroked her thigh, warm little trails of sensation down the back of her leg. His touch was so comforting, and she hated what she had to do next.

"But you know all that." She focused on the memories of what had come during those "gone" years that Mike didn't know about, so that she could get through it without breaking down again. She relayed it as a reporter would: emotionless and matter-of-factly. It was the only way she'd manage without falling to pieces.

"Steve wanted children, but not right away. He wanted us both to work for a while longer. Wait until we could afford it better. I was driving the highway one night on my way home from a night class and a deer jumped on to the road in front of me. I swerved, but there was traffic and I had to snap the wheel back. I hit the deer and put the car off the road, hitting a tree."

His hand stopped moving. Her heart beat a little faster, knowing what was coming and fearing his reaction, wondering if it would be dismay, disappointment, repulsion. None of those were things she wanted him to feel about her.

"When I woke up, I was in the hospital, in intensive care. I'd ruptured my spleen; had internal injuries. It wasn't for a few days that I finally heard what they'd done to me in the OR. I'd had a perforated uterus. They..." Her voice broke a little but she summoned her strength and carried on until the end. "They did a hysterectomy."

Now that it was out, she swallowed against the hard lump of tears lodged solidly in her throat. She'd done it. She'd said the words, but it didn't make her feel better. All it did was make it more real than it had been in a long, long time. It was the death of hope.

With dread she looked up at him.

Mike's hand had left her leg and was covering his mouth. He was clearly shocked, staring at her with a mix of dismay and disbelief.

His fingers scraped down over his jaw and chin. "You never told anyone? Not ever?"

"Steve stayed with me through recovery, but nothing was the same. We just...fell apart. He wanted things I couldn't give him." *Like you want things I can't give you,* she thought. She'd never wanted to have that feeling again—the encompassing, true feeling of utter failure. Of feeling like less than a whole woman. It had eaten her up after the accident and now it threatened to do so again. She made herself go on, to finish it and get it over with.

"Steve filed for divorce. He didn't want a wife who was damaged. Nothing fit into his plans anymore, you see. He'd had it all worked out, and suddenly nothing made sense, and he saw it as my fault. I came home. And I've tried to..." She stopped. Two tears dropped from her lashes on to her lap as she stared at the material there, willing herself to hold it together.

"The bottom line is, I can't have children, Mike. Those babies you're picturing? I'll never be able to give them to you."

Moments of heavy silence followed, until Mike stood up. He paused. "I don't know what to say."

But what he didn't say said everything for him. She felt his withdrawal in the cool night air. He was pulling away from her, just like she knew he would. He could say all he wanted about being sorry for leaving her in the past, but this moment was the truth she had always known.

"I know this is a shock to you."

His face was flat, devoid of any expression at all. "I saw the scar last night, but I thought it had been from when you had your appendix out."

"No. It's all from my internal injuries. I didn't even have a say...I just woke up and it was gone."

"I'm sorry," he got out, then abruptly turned, walking away towards the barns, his steps quickening the further away he got.

He was doing what she'd expected. Leaving. Just like before. Without a word of ending. But it didn't stop how much it hurt to watch him go.

Everything in her wanted to go after him.

But she couldn't. She knew she didn't have the right.

CHAPTER 9

She'd put it off long enough.

Day after tomorrow was Thanksgiving, and Grace hadn't been to Circle M since the night she'd told Mike about her accident. Nor had he called. Alex was home from the hospital now and the last of the leaves were struggling to stay on the trees in the October chill.

She took her purse from the hook and grabbed her car keys. It was no less than she'd expected, after all. He didn't need to say the words for her to know. She'd already felt like half a woman for years now. And she cared about Mike too much to pretend to be something she was not. She needed to get back to building her life again. Only this time she'd make the right decisions.

Before she lost her courage again, she locked the house and hopped into her car. It was high time she got back to work. She owed the garage another two hundred dollars and change, and then she'd be free and clear. But financially, it didn't spell the end of demands. Impending winter meant higher heating bills. Now that the baby was born, Alex would be itching to take the books back over within a few months. And then Grace wouldn't have to worry about running into Mike so much. It was bad enough that he was stuck in her thoughts night and day.

She turned the key in the ignition. Only to be rewarded by a constant clicking sound.

"You've got to be kidding me," she growled at the car. "Start, dammit!"

She tried again, but nothing.

The last time she'd had car trouble Mike had literally ridden to her rescue, but he wasn't there to save her anymore. He'd run, the way she knew he would. His silence said everything. She was back to relying on herself. And that was just what she was going to do.

She went back inside and called the garage. Thirty long minutes later Phil was there to give her a boost. With Mike in the passenger seat of the truck.

What in the world was he doing here?

Phil popped the hood while Mike hung back a bit. Grace put her hands in her pockets. Of all ways she'd thought they'd meet next, it wasn't this way.

"Hey Mike," Phil called, "turn it over, will you?"

Mike sent her a long, complicated glance and then moved to get in the driver's side of the car, dutifully turning the key.

"Again?"

Still, there was nothing but a recurring clicking sound from under the hood.

"She's dead, alright."

Mike got back out of the car. "I'll get the spare from the truck, then."

Grace followed him. He wore the usual jeans and boots but had eschewed his cowboy hat, leaving his head bare. "What are you doing here?"

Mike's eyes fell on her. "I was at the garage picking up a part for Connor when you called. Phil was coming out alone and I thought he could use a hand."

That was all, then. Grace looked away as Mike took a new battery to Phil and their two deep voices blended as they spoke. Mike had been there anyway and was being helpful. The way he always was. The closeness she'd felt between them before was gone.

It was a new beginning, and she should have been happy that he wasn't avoiding her any longer. They could perhaps start rebuilding their friendship. She knew it was what she *should* want. But she could still feel what it had been like to have him surround her, skin to skin. Forgetting wasn't going to be easy.

The engine roared to life this time, and Mike got out, leaving it running and the door open.

"You're all set now, Grace." Phil wiped his hands on a rag from his pocket. "You can catch up with me later."

"Thanks, Phil." She tried to sound grateful, but instead felt only frustration.

He probably wouldn't charge her for coming out to the house. But there was still the cost of the battery that would be added to her bill. Something else on the never-ending list of not getting ahead.

Mike went back to Phil's truck and Grace's eyes followed him. He was cold, so cold. So distant. And she'd done that. With Phil here, there was no way they could talk. And he obviously wasn't seeking her out to put things right. She squared her shoulders. There was no sense weeping about it. What was done was done.

She went up to the driver's side window. "Thanks, guys. I appreciate you both coming out to help." She said the words to them both, but her eyes clung to Mike's.

"You're welcome," Phil answered. Mike lifted a finger carelessly, only to realize his hat wasn't there. Normally she'd have teased him, but not now. It was almost as if there was too much between them, weighing them down, making smiles and light comments impossible.

With a wave, Phil was gone.

She got into her running car and headed towards the ranch. At least she knew Mike wouldn't be there since he was running errands in town.

From the outside, Windover looked exactly the same, but inside, it was a changed place. Grace could feel it as soon as she walked in the house. Alex was home again, and there was newborn evidence everywhere. In the kitchen it was a bouncy seat on the top of the counter. She passed the laundry room and saw a basket of tiny blue clothes next to a small bottle of baby laundry detergent. All reminders of a life she wouldn't have. She went into the study and shut the door.

Get in, get it done, and get out, she thought, settling into the chair and booting up the computer. If she could get this finished, she wouldn't have to come back for a few weeks. She dreaded seeing Mike now, knowing he was going to look at her differently. She didn't want to see that look of disappointment. Perhaps space and a little time would make it easier, instead of the raw wound it was now.

A knock on the door startled her away from her spreadsheet and her head swiveled to the doorway.

"Alex! Shouldn't you be resting?"

Alex stepped inside. "Are you kidding? I've spent weeks in bed. It's a relief to be up and about and thirty pounds lighter." She smiled at Grace. "I really just wanted to come in and ask if you stay for a cup of tea with me after you finished. Gram's taken Maren to Millie's to make pies for the church sale and Connor's out with Mike."

At the mention of Mike's name, Grace averted her eyes. "I should finish up in another few minutes."

A thin cry echoed from upstairs and Alex smiled. "Oops, take your time. The boss is awake." She slipped from the room and Grace heard her go upstairs, her soft voice soothing the baby.

When Grace finished, she packed up the things and left everything on the desk. The way Alex was bouncing back, she might want to take over again anytime. She'd miss the money, but maybe it would be easier for them both to simply move on if she wasn't around anymore.

She went into the kitchen. It was empty, but she moved to the patio doors anyway, looking out over the vast, brown landscape that dipped to the foot of the mountains. They'd had snow at the higher elevations, and the peaks were pristine white against the piercing blue of the sky. Two figures moved off to the left. Connor and Mike on horseback, she realized. She knew her car was visible from the barns, and even knowing they were leaving things unspoken, Mike hadn't sought her out. It hurt, even though she knew she had no right to be mad. She'd slept with him without telling him the truth; he'd responded by baring his heart to her. She couldn't blame him for being angry about it.

She turned from the window and went looking for Alex, finding her in the living room. She halted at the door, instantly embarrassed to find Alex nursing Jamie in the rocking chair. "Oh, I'm sorry."

Alex looked up. "Don't be. Come on in." She smiled at Grace.

Grace took a seat in the chair to Alex's left. She had no sisters, so wasn't accustomed to seeing someone breastfeed, let alone be so relaxed and casual about it. Even though she could see very little between the baby's head and the flannel receiving blanket tucked around him.

"Are you okay, Grace?"

Grace looked up but didn't know what to say. Her eyes met Alex's. She'd gone so long without trusting anyone with the secrets of her heart, but her emotions had been so up and down this fall that suddenly they were all so overwhelming. And her relationship with Alex had grown over the last months. She'd let the secret out once and felt the undeniable urge to unburden herself to someone who might not run away. She knew she could trust Alex.

Alex misinterpreted her silence, withdrawing. "I'm sorry if I'm overstepping."

"No, no, of course not," Grace assured her. "I'm just not used to talking about it, that's all."

"I thought you could use a female perspective on whatever's going on between you. Neither one of you is happy."

Grace tensed, unsure of what to say. "My relationship with Mike isn't like yours with Connor."

"But the other night, he went after you and brought you home. I know you two have gotten closer lately."

"Not anymore. I sort of fixed that the other night."

"You argued?"

"Not exactly...but we talked. I think it's safe to say Mike isn't interested in who I turned out to be."

Jamie's head drooped slightly, and Alex looked down, an affectionate chuckle escaping her lips. "He fell asleep." With a finger she wiped a dribble of milk from the corner of his mouth.

Deftly she put everything back in place and wrapped him up in his blanket, rocking the chair gently. "Mike is crazy about you, Grace. We weren't wrong at the hospital, were we? Something happened."

Grace nodded as the words came spilling out. "Yes, something happened. The night you had Jamie. But I did it for the wrong reasons, and now he knows, and he walked away from me and it's just all gone wrong."

"I don't understand."

Grace trusted Alex, as a woman and as a friend. She took a breath. "When I was twenty, I had an accident and they had to do a hysterectomy. You know what that means. It spelled the end of my marriage. The night Connor rushed you to the hospital and you had Jamie...that was the first time I'd been in a hospital since the accident.

I was feeling vulnerable and fragile and didn't want to be alone...so I... I wasn't."

Understanding dawned in Alex's eyes. "But Mike would understand that."

"He didn't know."

"About the hospital?"

"About the accident, about me not being able to have children, none of it."

Understanding dawned in Alex's eyes. "Until we opened our big mouths when you came to visit. Oh, we prattled on about having babies and teasing the two of you, and all the time you were hurting. I'm so sorry."

"No! Don't be! It's not your fault. You couldn't have known, and you were right. Things were happening. But I was feeling raw, and I knew I had to tell Mike and then someone mentioned babies and I just couldn't take it anymore. I should have told him sooner. Oh Alex, he was so caring, thinking I was upset about maybe getting pregnant. But you have to understand." She met Alex's eyes evenly. "Until that night, I hadn't told anyone. Not even my parents."

"And what happened?"

"We came back here, and I told him everything. He just walked away from me. Didn't say a word. Just turned and walked into the barns and left me sitting there all alone."

"Connor mentioned he drove you home and that you'd been crying. But he's not like me. I meddle. I think it's a requirement of motherhood."

"Mike is really mad at me."

He's surprised, that's all," she countered.

"No, not surprised. Well, maybe he is, but he's more disappointed. I know that. I've known Mike a long time. We dated once, and he hurt me badly. He's apologized for all of it, and instead of things working out I've thrown a whole monkey wrench into the works."

She ran a hand through her hair. "He pictures himself having the family he never had before. He's told me so. And I can't give it to him. I let things go on between us all the while knowing how he'd react. So he's not to blame in this. I am."

"And that had better be the last time I heard you blaming yourself for anything. It was an accident, Grace."

"I don't know when I would have told him. We seemed to argue so often, and then things started happening and is there ever a right time to spring news like that on someone? Oh, I've messed things up big time."

Alex adjusted the baby. "Have you spoken to Mike since?"

Grace shook her head. "No." She sighed. "My battery died this morning, and he was at the garage when I called. He came out with Phil and they put in a new one, but he was like a stranger."

Alex muttered something about stupid men under her breath. "We're having dinner here on Monday. I want you to come."

"You should enjoy your holiday. You don't need our *atmosphere* getting in your way. Right now, it might be better for us to keep our distance from each other and move on. So we don't hurt each other further."

"Nonsense. The longer you leave things without even seeing each other, the worse it's going to get. We're eating at one. Where else are you going to go, hmmm?"

Grace started to speak but Alex cut her off. "If you say home alone, I'm going to come over and shake some sense into you."

Grace's stomach fluttered at the thought of being in the same room as Mike. What in the world would they say to each other? Would he say anything at all?

But then...losing Mike's friendship was a difficult pill to swallow. Perhaps Alex was right. If they got this first meeting over with, perhaps they could start putting back together the friendship they'd had over the years. Maybe that was more important than anything else.

"Oh, all right. Only if Johanna's making cranberry stuffing."

At Alex's raised eyebrows, Grace laughed. "*Everyone* knows about Mrs. Madsen's famous stuffing."

"I'm putting Jamie to bed now, and we'll have that cup of tea." She rose from the rocker and gave Grace's arm a squeeze on the way by. "Thank you for telling me, Grace," she said softly. "I know it wasn't easy. But take it from one who knows. Finally trusting someone with your secrets is the real way to start healing. Things are going to get better. You just remember that."

······●··

It sure didn't feel like anything was healing. Grace stood on the front porch of Windover, holding a scalloped glass bowl of coleslaw and too scared to ring the bell.

What would he say? How would he look?

How would he look at her? Happy to see her? She doubted it. Uncomfortable, surely.

"You waiting for the butler?"

Connor's voice came from behind her, and she jumped. "Just being chicken."

"Today's a day for turkey, not chicken. Besides, it's just dinner. There's nothing that's been done that can't be fixed."

Oh, but there was. She couldn't take back time; the accident, the operation, or how she'd slept with Mike before telling him the truth. She couldn't repair the damage done by those things. But she smiled weakly. Connor was only trying to help. She wondered how much Mike had told him. Being men, probably very little.

"I can smell it out here," she admitted, smiling at him.

"Then let's eat," he said, rubbing his hands together with anticipation.

Grace laughed as he opened the door.

"It's about time you came in," Alex scolded, wagging a finger at her husband before bustling around the kitchen once more. "You need to wash up and the turkey is going to come out any minute for you to carve."

"Yes, dear," he answered cheekily, heading for the bathroom and soap and water. Grace put her bowl of salad on the counter as Johanna put Maren in her booster seat. She hung her coat on the row of hooks by the front door and was just turning back to ask Alex if she could help with anything when Mike turned the corner into the kitchen.

They both halted and stared across the table at each other. Grace swallowed as they stood there like idiots. He'd obviously come in and showered. His hair lay thickly against his head, a couple of curls springing forward as they dried. His face was smooth and freshly shaved, the red shirt he wore neat and pressed. Grace realized suddenly that red was his favorite color. He wore it more than any other.

Finally Mike spoke first. "Happy Thanksgiving, Grace."

She tugged at the hem of her sweater. She wanted to say *I'm sorry* and a million other things to him, but instead merely answered, "Happy Thanksgiving."

"Mike, will you light the candles? Grace, if you could put the rolls on, we're ready to eat." Alex issued last minute instructions.

When the table was loaded everyone sat down, baby Jamie snoozing contentedly in a Moses basket on the counter.

Alex asked Connor to say the blessing. Belatedly Grace realized that Alex was playing matchmaker even with seating arrangements. Alex and Connor sat at the head and foot. Johanna sat on one side, supposedly to help Maren with her dinner, which left Mike and Grace to fill out the other side. To make matters worse, everyone was joining hands. She gripped Alex's on her right and after a prolonged second, Mike took her left hand in his.

Just that much...that simple touch...told her that no matter how she'd blown things apart the other night, they were far from over— at least on her part. Mike meant more to her. As his hand covered hers firmly, she realized that Mike was *everything*. She had to try to find a way to rebuild their friendship. It was all she could have now, she knew that. But he was too important to let their connection go completely.

The blessing was over, and the kitchen was filled once more with chatter and the clattering of silverware against china. Grace dutifully filled her plate with the traditional dinner: turkey, stuffing, snowy mashed potatoes with a puddle of rich gravy, bright orange carrots. There was her coleslaw and cranberry sauce, and a traditional Scandinavian turnip casserole.

She realized her folly when she attempted to swallow the first bite. She had a plate loaded with food and no inclination to actually eat it. Beside her, Mike bumped her elbow as he buttered a fresh roll. She shivered. She wanted to forget the food and touch him. Put a hand on his warm thigh, strong beneath the stiff denim, and feel the reassurance of his body close to hers. When had he become her comfort? She wasn't sure, but it was true. She'd come to lean on him. And she felt the absence of that closeness acutely, especially now when she felt like everything was falling apart.

She managed to get through the meal and got up to help Johanna with dessert. Without asking, she put a slice of warm apple pie with ice cream on a plate, and then squeezed another piece of pumpkin beside it. Johanna started with the coffee pot while Grace served the pie.

Mike's face split into a wide smile when she placed the plate in front of him. He looked up, for the first time his expression unguarded. "How did you know?"

She smiled back. "I've known you for nearly twenty years. Of course I knew."

His gray-blue eyes warmed and for the second time she longed to apologize. For a minute it seemed he wanted to say something. The moment drew out and Grace realized no one else had pie yet. She turned back to the counter but felt sure his eyes lingered on her.

The coffee pot was drained and a second put on; Jamie woke up and Alex disappeared to change and feed him. While she was gone, Grace and Johanna started on the massive cleanup. For Alex to host such a dinner so soon after delivering was ambitious, even with Johanna's help. Grace was determined Alex be spared the dishes.

Connor took Maren upstairs for her afternoon nap while Grace loaded the dishwasher and Johanna ran water in the sink for what wouldn't fit in the dishwasher racks. Mike, the odd man out, looked after clearing the table linens and taking the leaf out of the pine table.

When the dishwasher was humming happily and the last of the things were tucked away, the afternoon was waning. Grace peeked in the living room to say her goodbyes, but the scene before her wrenched her heart completely.

Connor sat in the corner of the sofa, one foot on the floor and the other along the cushions. Alex sat in the lee of his legs, resting against him, her head turned to his shoulder. And Jamie lay on her chest, his tiny head facing Grace so that she could see the perfectly formed lips and the eyelashes lying against his cheeks. All three were sleeping.

Connor's right arm covered Alex and his hand rested on the tiny foot of his son.

It was so perfect that Grace stared at them with a lump in her throat. It was something she and Mike would never have, and with the exception of the end of her marriage, never had she felt the absolute desolation of the knowledge as acutely. Finally, feeling like she was intruding, she backed out of the room and went to get her purse. There was nothing more for her here. And now, with her emotions in so fragile a place, she really wanted to avoid having to deal with Mike and all the feelings she was having trouble holding inside.

"Heading out already?"

Mike's warm voice stopped her, and she turned to see him in the hall behind her. Why now, when she was feeling as low as she possibly could? It took great fortitude for her to try to smile normally and reply, "Everyone is resting. I thought it was as good a time as any to sneak away."

"Would you be sneaking away from me, then?"

He wasn't smiling, wasn't teasing. His eyes probed hers, asking for time and for the briefest of seconds, she wanted to lift her hand and smooth it along his jaw.

It was an honest question and deserved an honest answer. She held his eyes with hers as she answered truthfully.

"Yes, I probably would be."

"I'm sorry about that."

He was apologizing to her? She didn't expect it and she knew they had to talk it out, even if the very idea frightened her, simply by acknowledging what needed to be faced. He had nothing to be sorry for.

"I'm the one who's sorry."

Still, he didn't move.

"I should get going," she continued.

"Why don't you take a walk with me first?"

Oh, how she wanted to. But there was a dangerous thing called hope and no matter how much she wanted to preserve their friendship, she knew that allowing herself to hope was a mistake. Dragging out all those feelings again was just opening a wound.

"Mike, I..."

"When do I ever take no for an answer?" He finally smiled. "Just a walk. It's a beautiful fall day, and we might not have many more this nice before winter's here for good. Cold front's coming in and we're in for some damp, cold weather."

She paused again and his casual smile faded. "Please Grace. I want us to talk."

She put down her purse. "All right. I'll go."

He took her coat and held it while she threaded her arms through the sleeves. His hands lingered just a moment on her shoulders, then he reached past her to open the door.

CHAPTER 10

Mike led her south of the barns through the pasture. Ever since she'd told him she couldn't have children, he couldn't figure out how he should react. He felt all sorts of things about it: hurt, anger, disappointment. For them both. But that wasn't her fault. It was his. He'd walked away, then hadn't attempted to make contact. He'd done exactly what he'd said he wouldn't. She'd been so cold to him today he knew she was angry and hurt. Even now, her mouth was set in a remote line and her eyes evaded looking at him at all. And hurting her further was the last thing he wanted to do.

He let the silence settle things for a while as their footsteps crunched through dead grass and dried leaves. He stopped and plucked a daisy, amazed that it still survived after the frosts they'd had. He stared at the white petals, then handed it to her silently. She took it, twisted the stem in her fingers, a small smile finally playing on her lips. It felt right, like she was more receptive to him and ready to talk, and he took her hand, guiding her to a huge boulder. She climbed up and sat on its flat top, pulling her knees up to her chest. Mike hopped up beside her.

"I'm sorry," he began as they both stared off at the valley that dipped to the southwest. He hadn't apologized to a woman since he'd begged for Mrs. Hawkins to keep him when he was nine, but he needed to say it a lot lately to Grace. The jagged line of the Rockies spread before them and Mike breathed deeply, searching for the words. "I shouldn't have walked away like that, and I'm sorry."

She didn't look at him. "I was wrong in not telling you before."

He turned slightly. God, she was strong, he realized. She'd dealt with her personal tragedy on her own, had come out still standing tall. Her hair blew back from her face in the westerly wind, her cheeks prettily pink in the cool fall air. The last thing she should be doing is blaming herself.

"Is that why you think I'm mad?"

"It's something you should have known before we slept together."

"And you think that's a deal breaker." He prodded her, trying to discover how she really felt about all of it. It was true. He was angry that she hadn't told him before, but not because they'd slept together first. With Grace, for the first time ever, it wasn't about sex. There had been women before and after her, but they hadn't been in his heart the way she was. It was about her, and he felt cheated that she hadn't trusted him with it.

"Isn't it? Can you say that you would have taken things that far if you'd already known?"

He hesitated. What if she was right? If he'd known in advance, would he have pursued her? Kissed her? Made love to her? He wanted to say yes, that it didn't matter, but he honestly couldn't. If he'd known she couldn't have children, he might have stepped back and thought about it long and hard before letting things develop.

"It doesn't matter if I would have or not, we did, and it's that we have to deal with," he evaded.

"You want things I can't give you, so what we did is really irrelevant. I don't blame you for walking away the other night. I expected it. That's why I put off telling you."

He turned away. She thought he was angry because she hadn't told him about her condition before they'd had sex. She couldn't be more wrong.

"I didn't walk away from you in anger, Grace," he answered. "I was shocked. It was not what I'd expected, and I didn't know how to handle it. But I wasn't mad, I promise you that." On the contrary. He'd ached for her. Her pain had been raw, fresh, and debilitating and he hadn't known what to do to help her. He knew he should have had the right things to say, but that had never been a strong point of character with him. He'd always been a man of plain words, not one that always had the right thing to say at the appropriate time.

He should have done something but at the time he couldn't escape the horrifying image of her lying in a hospital bed.

Or the red anger of knowing the man she'd married had used it as an excuse to end their marriage. He hadn't known what to do with those feelings churned up inside, but he knew one thing...he didn't want her to have to deal with them. He'd walked away.

Grace held back the tears but couldn't keep her chin from wobbling. "Disappointed, then."

"Grace." He took her cold hand in his, couched it between his palms. His skin warmed hers and she clung to the sound of his voice, even and strong.

"I am not disappointed in you. What happened wasn't your fault and nobody blames you. You have to know that."

She finally looked up at him, her eyes bright with anguish at his kind tone. How could he not be disappointed with her when she was with herself? It was so clear to her that Mike wanted things she couldn't give him. She used her pain like armor to keep him away, save herself from further hurt.

"Steve blamed me. Enough that he moved on to a whole woman."

"He said that? A whole woman?" Grace watched Mike's fingers flex and bunch by his sides. "Forget Steve." Mike scowled. "Steve doesn't warrant your consideration. You are no less of a woman. Believe me."

A hint of a sad smile tipped her lips. "Thank you for that. But Steve isn't the point, either. I've seen your house. I know that you built it with a family in mind. And I also know how much that means to you." She lifted her face to the mountains. "I know how you grew up, Mike, and I took advantage of that."

He turned his head away, but not before she saw his expression change. For a moment he almost looked guilty.

"You think you took advantage of me." He snorted out a chuckle.

"I slept with you knowing it was temporary. There can't be anything long term between us. You know that." Her heart cracked a little even as she said the words. It was true; but saying it made it seem more permanent.

Mike stepped off the rock and walked away, shaking his head. He spun back. She watched him evenly, gathering all the strength she had to keep from crying. She knew things about Mike that very few people knew, and one was that he'd had his share of people casting him aside. She didn't want him to think she was doing that. She was setting him free to find the life he really wanted.

She longed to throw herself in his arms but knew it would ultimately be unfair. Turning him away now would be less hurtful than what would happen if they ignored the facts. So she watched him, trying to accept the inevitable. Hoping he would too so she could hold her head high and lick her wounds in private.

"Sleeping together was my fault. I knew you were upset, and I did it because I wanted you. If anyone took advantage, it was me. I should never have expected you to give me more."

Just when she thought she couldn't hurt any more. He thought she didn't want him? Was he crazy? He was all she'd dreamed of for such a long time she wasn't sure she could forget how. Wasn't sure she even wanted to.

All the resentment she'd harbored over the years bubbled over. But she held her temper. If it had to end now, she didn't want it to be with a drawn-out argument. They'd done their share of that this fall.

"I mean, I'm not that guy," he continued. His voice held an edge of "I don't care" attitude. "I'm not the kind of man a woman loves, I know that. I made the mistake of thinking there was something more between us. But I was wrong."

She stared at him, watching him withdraw into himself. He was shrugging this off like it was nothing, but she knew better. That was what he thought this was about? Not being lovable? Not being wanted?

God, would he never get it?

"This isn't about you!" Her knees dropped down and she braced her hands on the gray stone. "This is about both of us wanting things that we can't give each other, don't you see that? I know how you grew up. I know you think you don't deserve love, and that's wrong. I get it, Mike. But your past doesn't matter to me. It never has! That isn't why, so don't brush this off as some fatal flaw you have!"

She knew he'd been tossed from one foster home to another. Always passed off to be someone else's problem until his cousin Maggie stepped in. Maggie had tried, everyone knew that, but she'd been young herself, and unprepared for a boy on the edge of manhood, invading her space. Grace remembered his face years ago when he'd casually tossed away the comments made about his childhood. He'd worn the same devil-may-care expression then, too. The one she knew hid a whole lot of pain. The one that told her he'd die before admitting she'd hurt his feelings.

The closest he'd ever come was when he'd found her crying in a back field, the place where a bunch of them gathered to party. To make her feel better, he'd revealed a few paltry slivers about what his young life had been like. And then he'd kissed her, and she'd dared to hope. She'd only dated the other boy to try to get Mike's attention.

She was now very well acquainted with what he'd felt back then— loneliness and utter inadequacy.

He couldn't know how much what he'd been through mirrored exactly how she felt about her marriage to Steve. She'd never measured up. How she'd tried to please him, live up to an ideal that didn't exist. And how could she possibly do that again? If it hurt leaving Mike now, how much would it kill her when he finally realized she'd never be what he truly wanted?

She gentled her voice. "You don't think I saw how lonely you were, or how much you longed for a real family?"

"Is that what you think this is about?" He backed away from her kindness, putting more distance between them. "I don't want your pity!"

His voice echoed down over the hill and to the valley, the words ringing in her ears. Indignation burned through her.

Nor did she want his. She hopped down from the boulder, squaring off against him. "And that's what I'm saying! We want different things! It's not wrong for you to want a family, and the home you never had! But don't you see? I can't give them to you!"

"I'm not asking you to carry my burdens for me!"

They were shouting at each other now, and she let the anger and frustration carry her. "That's pretty funny, considering you've tried running my life for the last two months!"

"We're back to that again?"

"Why are we arguing again?" She exploded with frustration.

"Because I care about you, dammit!"

Her chest heaved with invigorated breathing, and she struggled to regain control. He cared, yes. But he hadn't once said he loved her.

And that was probably for the best after all. Especially if things were ending here.

"Then care enough about me to be my friend. That's all we can be."

His gaze met hers, long and complicated. Her heart pounded, wanting him to say the words, even though she knew it would be a mistake. Wanting him to say he would fight for her, even though she kept pushing him away. That he would fight for them.

She watched as the anger drained away from him. His cheeks relaxed, he stopped pursing his lips. But now, with his frustration gone, he simply looked sad and empty.

Mike's voice was soft as he answered. "I'll always be your friend, Grace, you know that."

Her breath hitched in her throat. Why, after everything, those words made her want to cry, she didn't know. She held on to the thin thread of control, swallowing several times and trying to exhale slowly.

The whole discussion had been a rollercoaster of ups and downs, understanding and anger, and Grace wanted off. When he held out his hand, she took it, let him pull her in and rested her head against his wide chest. His heartbeat was there against her ear, strong and fast. His arms circled her, protecting, soothing.

After several minutes, she finally spoke. "I was afraid we'd lost this."

His heart leaped.

"Lost what?" He tilted his chin down, gazing at the top of her head and the tip of her nose.

"The other morning...you were so cold. I don't think I could stand it if I lost your friendship, Mike. It means a lot, knowing you're here when I need you. I've always known it. Always."

"I couldn't say anything to you then, not in front of Phil. I wasn't sure how you'd react, but I had to know you were okay."

She pulled out of his arms, looking up. He looked so much shorter, so much more approachable without his hat, she realized. Although the cowboy hat lent another sort of allure to him. "I thought you were done with me for good. I thought I'd lost a friend as well as..." She paused.

"As well as a lover?"

"Y-yes."

His gaze seared into hers, but his words belayed what his eyes were saying.

"It's getting dark. You should get back."

"You're not coming?"

"No, you go ahead. I'm going to check the west pasture."

He was avoiding her already, she realized, and despite their agreement to be friends, she knew he was distancing himself. It was what was right, she supposed. Only it hurt more than she'd ever imagined. She didn't want to go, but there wasn't anything left to say. At least this time they'd ended it with words.

"All right. Happy Thanksgiving, Mike."

"You, too."

She turned on a heel and walked away. She didn't look back, couldn't. She didn't want to know if he'd walked away too, or if he was still standing there watching her go.

· · · ● · ● · · · ·

When he couldn't hear her footsteps anymore, he turned back around. She was already at the gate. With a sigh, he dropped down on the boulder, resting his elbows on his knees.

Damn.

Now that she was gone, he could think about what had just happened, because in the thick of it emotions had gotten in the way.

In his mind he went over and over what had been said...and what hadn't.

Her anger had only masked her pain, he realized that now. And he'd played right along with it. As much as the spunky, independent Grace had driven him crazy, he would have given anything to have her back in place of the wounded spirit he knew she was trying to hide.

He wasn't angry that she didn't tell him, and he wasn't disappointed in her. That much, at least, was clear. It was equally clear to him that she *was* angry, and disappointed in how things turned out. And she had every right to be.

The sun dipped lower in the autumn sky and a chill settled, seeping through the fabric of his shirt. He chafed his hands together, keeping them warm. There were some things he hadn't been able to say. It was obvious she was hurting, and he didn't need to add to her burden. But the truth of it was, knowing how much pain she was in, knowing why, he felt completely and utterly helpless.

She had no uterus. That was the plain, ugly truth. There would be no babies for her, not ever. It had cost her not only children but her husband, and now she thought it had cost her him. She was blaming herself and he could do nothing to fix it. And that was what he knew how to do. Fix things. But nothing he could do could change what had happened to her. He could not make this go away for her and it was the one thing he hated the most.

He'd wanted to say, "Let me help you," but he didn't know how. How in the world could he make that right for her? What was done was done. He realized she was taking their relationship down from where it had gone and leaving it as friends only, and he resented it even as he understood why she was doing it. She was giving him an out and trying to preserve their long-time friendship. She was turning him away.

His jaw clenched against the pain of it. Just friends. Was that all he was good for, then? And yet, he didn't have the heart to be angry with her for it.

He had been cold, but only because he'd felt incredibly awkward and guilty for walking away when she'd needed him. In hindsight he should have stayed, tried to help her through it, made sure she got home all right. Instead he'd left it up to Connor. Like a coward, Mike had hidden with his horses until Connor got home. The next morning, Connor had eyed him speculatively over the breakfast table, but Mike had remained stonily silent. He didn't like that about himself.

He hadn't put all this in motion to just walk away now. She had healing to do, and he didn't want to press the issue right at this moment. But she wouldn't get rid of him that easily.

He stood up, suddenly seeing the daisy he'd picked sitting wilted on the stone beside him. He picked it up, the head of the flower flat on the palm of his hand. The daisy was strong, and resilient. Just like Grace. He tucked it in his shirt pocket.

She needed to be convinced.

What she needed was wooing.

·· • • • •• • • • ··

Daisies suddenly appeared everywhere she went.

On the dash of her car when she left Mrs. Cooper's after cleaning her house. Tucked in the handle of her screen door. On the desk at Windover when she went to do payroll. One every day, until she began looking for it. Wondering where it would show up next. Wondering why.

She had no doubt as to the who, however. She knew it was Mike. He'd given her the first blossom on Thanksgiving and there'd been one every day since. What she didn't understand was why he was doing it.

He wanted children, had said the words to her. And knowing what he knew, why was he still pursuing her? It was ridiculous. He had to know it was over between them. She wanted him to stop this nonsense so they could keep the good memories of what had been.

She stopped at the grocery store, and then paid a visit to Phil. When she left the garage, it was with a sense of relief and freedom. Her repair bill was finally paid. It was one less thing for her to worry about, a small detail in the overall scheme of things but something positive to cling to. And she'd done it on her own.

It was nearly dinner time, and she realized there had not been a daisy today. She quelled the disappointment stirring in her heart. When had she started expecting them? She wasn't sure, but as she drove home, she knew that at some point she'd started looking for them to show up. And as much as she wanted him to cease it, she couldn't help but look for where the next one would be.

Perhaps her lack of communication had finally got through to him and he was stopping. It was what she wanted, right?

Twilight was settling in early these days and already the afternoon was starting to dim when she pulled into her yard. She grabbed her bag of groceries and went up the back steps, pausing at the mailbox to pick up the day's mail.

And there was her daisy.

She didn't know where he was getting them. It was too cold for them to be blooming wild anymore; he had to be getting them from a florist. The stem of it was taped to a tiny envelope. She slid her finger underneath the flap and pulled out a plain card. It was adorned only by Mike's rough handwriting, and like the man, it was of few words.

Saturday night, seven p.m. Housewarming at Mike's, Circle M Ranch. BYOB, music and food provided.

Not a request for a personal assignation, then. She wasn't sure if she was relieved or not. And for a moment she considered not going. But then she lifted the flap on the card and he'd scrawled two words. *Please come.*

She knew she couldn't ignore the personal request. And she also knew she was incredibly curious about how his house turned out.

She probably would regret it, but as she went inside, she was already planning what she was going to wear.

CHAPTER 11

The lights were blazing from Mike's windows, the drive filled with cars and trucks of various sizes when Grace pulled up and killed the engine.

Even from the distance down the lane, she could hear the steady thump of a bass drum coming from the garage. The huge double door was up, and she could tell by the sound erupting that the band was set up there, with the flat, concrete floor acting as a dance floor for those so inclined. Normally she'd be excited about this type of party, so common among the community. But tonight she felt alone, outside the festivities. The fact that it was carefree, no-one-can-tie-me-down Mike that was celebrating a new house made everything seem more odd.

Grace made her way past the garage, lifting a hand to wave at a few people, offering a smile as she balanced a plastic container on her palm. Normally she was upbeat and relaxed at this sort of function, but not tonight. When she got to the door, she pulled her hand away from the knob. She had the feeling she should turn back and go home. She shouldn't be here. There was no point. The last time she'd been at a similar gathering, she'd made a complete fool of herself with Mike and had set this whole thing in motion. Now look where that had gotten her. Hurt and confused.

She was about to turn away when the door flew open, and Alex stood there with baby Jamie in her arms.

"Finally!" Alex's grin was from ear to ear. "We were wondering when you'd show up!"

There was no turning back now.

She stepped inside and followed Alex to the kitchen. Because the other woman carried the baby, people moved aside for her to pass, and before Grace could protest, she was standing before Mike, who was dumping potato chips into a bowl.

He smiled, and her heart caught.

"Hey, Grace. Glad you could make it." He picked up the snacks, still grinning easily in her direction.She'd steeled her spine, prepared herself for seeing him again. Had given herself a stern talking-to about it being over and them being friends. She'd thrown away every single daisy that had been delivered to her, after a suitable period of admiration. And she'd been so sure that they could go back to their old relationship.

Then he said her name and smiled and it was all out the window. She cared for him as much as she ever had. Her heart fluttered and her hands ached to reach out and touch him, to lose herself in his arms.

Alex was watching her strangely, so she pasted on a smile and held out the container. "No potted plant from me, you'd kill it in a week," she joked weakly. "But I brought something else instead."

He put down the bowl in his hands and reached for the white plastic. "What is it?"

"Open it."

He lifted the lid and sighed appreciatively. "Caramel apple pie."

"I didn't think you'd do much baking for yourself, and I know what your appetite is like."

His eyes met hers and she felt the blush creep up her cheeks. Appetites indeed. A memory flashed through her mind, one of soft skin and sighs in the dark light of pre-dawn. Her pulse jumped. Oh, this was silly! She had to at least try to keep things normal.

"Your party is hoppin'." Grace made her voice sound jaunty, keeping the strain from it. "Live band and everything."

"We've got a good turnout. Not just for me but for Circle M, too."

"Work in everything," Alex pretended to gripe. "Can't just have a party for party's sake. He and Connor have angles working you can't even imagine." She lifted Jamie up so he was face to face with her. "Speaking of, let's find your daddy and get you home, little man."

Alex put a hand on Grace's arm. "We're going to take the kids home with Johanna, but we'll be back."

Grace looked up at Mike. "They are obscenely happy."

"Yes, they are." His pale eyes searched hers and again wishes snuck in, ones she knew she had to right to have.

"Excuse me for a few minutes, okay?" He put his fingers on her arm. "I've got a few things to look after. But I'll be back."

He disappeared. Grace took the opportunity to grab a can of pop from a cooler sitting in the corner of the large kitchen. She wandered over to the bay window. Now, in the dark, the view was black, with only the hulking shadows of trucks and cars viewable.

The house was crowded, stifling. She grabbed a handful of pretzels from a low table and wandered out to the garage.

The band was playing something fast and couples were moving and turning in an East Coast Swing. Grace laughed as she saw Connor swirling Alex under his arm. On the sidelines, Johanna held the baby and Mike held Maren in his arms, the black-haired tot clapping her chubby hands along to the rousing music. Mike caught her watching, smiled and shrugged as if to say, "What could I do?" Seeing him holding the little girl only reinforced the knowledge that they'd done the right thing, breaking it off. He'd always want children of his own, and she'd hate to look into his eyes down the road and see resentment there for the babies she'd never be able to give him.

When the song ended, Connor took Maren from Mike's arms and the family left the concrete floor for the crisp fall air outside. Mike threaded his way through the crowd until he was at Grace's side.

"They were all set to leave, and then Connor decided he wanted to dance first."

"Connor's changed so much since Alex came into his life." Grace gazed at their departing figures. Connor held Maren in one arm, but his free hand was clasped in Alex's.

"Love will do that to a man," Mike answered.

Grace's gaze darted to his. But before she could think, he grabbed her hand and tugged. "Come on. It's time we danced."

The band struck up an old Vince Gill tune, and Mike pulled her into his arms for a waltz. Grace's breath grew shallow and she struggled to relax, her feet finding the three-count rhythm with his lead. The last time she'd danced with Mike she'd been drinking and that was how this whole thing had started. It had seemed harmless at the time, flirting and innuendoes. But Mike wasn't harmless. He was devastating.

His feet shuffled with the other couples, guiding her across the cold concrete floor. His hand was wide and firm along the hollow of her back as the words of the old song touched her, struck by their poignancy. She didn't have to wait for love to find her; she already knew. Knew because suddenly, in the space of a moment, love was being held in Mike's arms. Strong and secure, a shoulder to lean on when life got to be too much. It wasn't a random thing that Mike was the first person she'd ever shared her burden with, even if by doing so she'd killed her chances to be with him. Tears stung the back of her eyes as she wished yet again that she could give him everything he wanted. What he deserved. Most of the time she'd been able to forget feeling so inadequate. It was only when faced with her growing feelings, of wanting things, that she felt more of a disappointment than ever before.

As the guitarist played a solo, his arms pulled her closer and his steps shortened, making their turns more intimate. His hand slid beneath the hem of her sweater, resting sweetly on the tender skin of her back.

Her body came alive where his fingers touched, where their bodies grazed and met through the movements of the dance. One night with Mike wouldn't be enough. She'd known it then and had denied it. If she'd known how this would have all transpired months ago when she'd propositioned him, would she still have said what she had? About him being a tiger in bed? There was so much more to him, and as much as it hurt her to know they had no future, she couldn't bring herself to be sorry that they'd had something that had burned so brightly before dying out.

She could always hold in her heart the memory of what it was like to once have been loved by Mike Gardner. It would have to be enough.

The song's final notes drifted out and voices started chattering again. Mike looked up at the singer, then back down at Grace.

"One more," he demanded, his hand still firm on her back. The music started, and for a moment Grace didn't recognize the old-fashioned sounding tune. Then it struck her, and she smiled wistfully.

It was deliberate ploy, but it touched her heart in ways she hadn't imagined.

It was the one-two-three rhythm of "I'll Give You a Daisy a Day, Dear". The sweetness of it filled her, the surprise of discovering Mike could be so sentimental. As they swirled around the makeshift floor, she rested her head in the hollow of his shoulder and let her body follow his like a shadow.

The band switched to an upbeat tempo and she heard Mike's voice, husky in her ear: "Come with me. I want to show you something."

He kept her hand in his, threading them through the other dancers and to the door of the house. The crowd inside had thinned, most now in the garage with the music or outside on the deck.

"You haven't seen the house since it was finished." They passed another couple in the foyer. "The decorating's still a bit sparse, but you'll get the idea."

Now that the throng had moved outside, Grace realized that there was very little in the living room. There was a coffee table and a single sofa, but no chairs, no knick knacks or pictures on the walls that made a house a home. In the kitchen was a dropleaf table with two chairs; the dining area was completely empty except for a temporary card table holding munchies and plastic bottles of pop for mixing drinks. Grace smiled to herself. Here was clearly a bachelor's pad, functional yet without the little touches. Yet the space was so well designed, she couldn't help but love it anyway. She felt guilty walking over the fine hardwood in her shoes. As they passed through the kitchen to the hallway, she ran her fingers over the glossy woodwork. Everything was so new, so fresh.

The bathroom door was open, the light on for guests, but he guided her past it, and past the other doors leading to the spare bedrooms. "They aren't decorated yet," he explained softly. "I wanted to get the other rooms done first."

At the end of the hall, he led her into his bedroom. A lamp burned in the corner, throwing a little circle of warm light into the space. It too was large and mostly empty except for a queen-sized bed and a plain maple dresser. A navy comforter was pulled up over the bed, slightly askew and a pillow crooked on the top.

It was lonely, Grace realized. She left him at the door and went to the ensuite, marveling at the white tile, the veined marble around the sink and the deep jetted tub. It was stunning, but somehow sterile. Like it hadn't been used. Waiting.

She went back out, turning out the light. "Your house is great, Mike. You must be so proud."

He shut the bedroom door, closing them in. "It's very plain, but there's a reason for that."

"There is?" He was walking closer and she tensed, sensing something unpleasant was coming which had to be ridiculous. Not after the way he'd touched her as they'd danced. There was nothing unpleasant in the whole evening. They'd been mending fences.

He stopped before her, and taking his hand from behind his back, held out a single daisy.

"I'm no good at decorating."

She laughed, a nervous giggle, belatedly reaching out to take the daisy. "Mike, you don't have to keep giving me flowers. Even a daisy a day." He had to have a standing order at the florist by now. "I'm not mad at you."

"Is that why you think I'm doing it?"

"Isn't it? Things haven't really been that great between us since…"

"Since the night we visited Alex at the hospital."

"Yes."

"It took me a while, and I know I've been, well, absent, I suppose. But I've figured out how to fix it."

"Oh Mike," she sighed, turning away. "I don't know how we'd even begin to really fix things."

He reached out and his hand gripped her forearm. He tugged, pulling her close, then tipping her chin up with a finger.

"This is a good place to start," he murmured. His eyes closed, the lashes fluttering on his skin as he placed his lips gently on hers.

"Like this," he whispered, kissing the corners of her mouth, each one like a warm drop of candle wax, soft, marking her, making her ache in every sensitive part of her body.

She wound her hands up and around his shoulders, her fingertips touching the coarse hair on the back of his neck as the daisy fell to the floor. Loving Mike could be so easy, so natural. Her lips opened, responding as he covered her mouth fully and drew her up against the tall, hard length of his body. He was what she wanted. What she craved. What she needed. He always had been.

His hands ran down her arms, finally gripping her fingers in his as he dragged his mouth away. "Don't you see, Grace?"

Her breath came in short, aroused gasps. "See what?"

Oh goodness. When he turned those gray eyes on her that way, she lost all her bearings. It had always been that way. His gaze plumbed hers earnestly, like he was waiting for an answer to an unasked question.

"Don't you see I built this for you? That it's waiting for you? For you and me?"

The room tipped, then righted itself as she stared at him.

"Built this for me?" She echoed it stupidly. "But...you started building it before we ever even...you broke ground the day you told me Alex was in hospital."

"And designed it before then."

"I don't understand."

He lifted one of her hands and pressed a kiss to it. "Did you think I hadn't noticed you before then? And the night we danced, and you said those things...I couldn't stop thinking about you. For the first time, I could see myself really settling. Not just with the ranch—the business was already going—but personally. I wanted to deserve you. I thought—after I'd made such a mess of things the first time—that it was over. And then you said those things and everything changed. I made *plans.*"

But Mike doesn't plan, she thought in a daze. "You planned this. The dating. The house. Everything."

It came out flatly and she saw the corners of his lips turn down in a frown. "I didn't orchestrate every movement, if that's what you mean," he replied tightly. "I just...I wanted...oh, dammit, I wanted you to have this. To have *me.*"

Panic left her cold. "Did it ever occur to you to ask me what I wanted?"

When he remained speechless, she backed away. This wasn't right. When she'd married Steve, he'd had their life planned out. He'd suggested the new job and the move to Edmonton. He'd found the perfect house. He'd been the one to want to wait to have children. And when he'd decided their marriage wasn't going to work anymore, he'd been the one to file for divorce.

And the moment she'd signed her name to the papers, she'd decided right then and there that no man would ever plan her life out for her again.

Yet that was exactly what she'd allowed Mike to do. He'd controlled the reins all along, she realized. And it had to stop here before they got even more hurt, if that were possible.

"Ask you?"

She gathered all the strength she had inside and wrapped herself in it for protection. "Did you expect me to be flattered, Mike? To fall at your feet and thank you for your devotion?"

From the incredulous expression on his face, she could tell that was exactly what he'd expected, and it infuriated her further.

"And the daisies? Was that your brilliant lead-up? Soften me up and then hit me with a grand gesture?"

His jaw hardened. "You do understand what I'm trying to say here, don't you Grace? And you're throwing it all back in my face."

"Ever since I started doing the books for Circle M you've thought it your *right* to run my life. To tell me where I can or can't work. Tried to pay my way. But not once did you think that you could have been insulting me!"

His head snapped up. "You feel insulted? Me wanting to be with you, building you a house, wanting to take care of you, that *insults* you?"

"Don't you respect me enough to let me make my own decisions?"

"This isn't about that!"

She began to pace, her shoes making dull thuds against the bare floor. "It's exactly about that! I went through this once already, Mike, and I won't do it again! Steve had our whole life mapped out, house, cars, kids when it was time...and when things didn't go according to plan, he left. I made up my mind then and there that I would never give anyone that control again! I make my own decisions. I run my own life. I don't need you to take care of me! I can't believe you thought this would be okay!"

"What should I have done then, Grace? Come to you months ago and told you I was designing a house? And that I wanted you in it, so could you please give me your input? That's ludicrous!"

He really didn't see that he'd done anything wrong, she realized. He still thought it was okay that he'd done all this without a word to her. "I already have a house. You might have considered that. And you might have considered telling me your feelings and asking mine before doing such a stupid thing as building a house for me."

His voice dripped ice. "And what would you have said to me, Grace? If I'd come to you and told you that I thought I was falling for you and I wanted to build us a house and have babies?"

Those last words were like cold steel slicing into her body, a low blow she hadn't thought he was capable of. "That's unfair. Knowing what you know...I can't believe you'd use that against me."

"I didn't know then, remember? For all I knew, until a few weeks ago, you could have, and probably wanted, children!"

"Because it was my business to tell!"

"And isn't it interesting, that when you finally did tell me, it was after we'd made love and you were scared to death!"

The room went deathly silent.

"What are you saying, Mike? That I used what happened to me?" The words were low, and carefully annunciated.

"Maybe that's exactly what I'm saying. You used it to hide from me. You take your injury and wear it like armor to keep anyone from getting too close. And look what happened the one time you let your guard down. We made love. We were as close as two human beings could be and that scared the life out of you. And you're back to hiding behind it again! Using it to hide what your real problem is!"

"Oh, please," she replied, the words ripe with contempt. "Please, tell me what my *problem* is."

Mike hooked his thumbs into his pockets. "Your problem, Grace, is that you're terrified. You're scared I can't love you enough. That eventually I'm going to leave like *he* did. Like *I* did before. You don't believe me when I say I'm in this for the long run. You think that someday I'll turn around and realize you aren't what I wanted after all. And so you hide behind what you think is real so that you don't have to deal with that."

When it was out he inhaled sharply, surprised he'd been callous— and courageous—enough to say all that. All the color drained from her face and tears streaked down her cheeks although her eyes never blinked. He watched the pain etch itself on her features as all he'd said sunk in, saw flickers of hatred burn in her eyes. But this time he wouldn't turn away. She could hate him, hit him, cry, whatever. But he wasn't backing down. This was too important. If nothing else, they had to take this back down to the basics, start over.

Her mouth opened and closed a few times, but no words came out. Finally, after several seconds, she pushed past him, wrenched open the door and flew down the hall.

He followed her with long strides, ignoring the curious stares from his guests. She ran out the front door and down the drive to her car. He paused on the front steps, his hands braced on the railing.

When he turned his head, he saw Alex and Connor staring up from the bottom of the stairs.

"Mike?"

He swallowed against the lump in his throat. He'd been too hard on her. He'd thought he'd been doing the right thing by telling her about the house.

He'd been very wrong.

He was sure of one thing, though. With his brutal honesty, he'd done enough damage for one night. For a lifetime.

"Go after her," Alex urged.

Connor said nothing. But when Mike looked in his friend's eyes, he knew Connor understood.

"Let her go," Mike said hoarsely, looking out over the road where her headlights flashed out of sight. "Nothing's going to fix this now."

Chapter 12

Mike gritted his teeth as Alex put her hands on her hips and said, "She's distraught. You should at least go after her."

"And say what, Alex? I can't fix this. She needs time. Time to figure out what she truly wants."

"Men!" Alex exploded. Connor gave her a warning glance, but she kept at Mike anyway.

He let her. It momentarily distracted him from remembering the crushed look on Grace's face. He hadn't meant to be cruel.

"She doesn't need *time*. She needs *you,* only you're too stupid to see it!"

Mike met Alex's eyes evenly. "I don't know how to help her. Lord knows I've tried. I don't know what else to do. All we end up doing is hurting each other more." He knew everything he'd said tonight had been excruciatingly painful and to say more would break their bond completely. That was the last thing he wanted.

Alex sighed, her face softening. She came up the steps to the landing and lifted a hand to his face, touching his cheek gently. "Love her, Mike. Just love her and everything else will fall into place."

With that she was gone.

Could it really be that easy?

Mike looked at Alex and Connor as they walked home through the shadows, the porch light from Windover guiding their way. He shook his head in wonderment. Connor had proposed to Alex on the same day he'd met her, and acknowledging that they'd grown to love each other had been a huge risk. But so obviously worth it. He ran his fingers through his hair. It was easier to build houses and make plans than to talk about emotions. But maybe that was what Grace needed. Maybe that was what they both needed in order to move past this.

· · · · · · · · · · ·

Grace pulled her knees closer to her chest, wrapping her arms around them. Very few people knew of this place, and she liked it that way. From the top of this hill she could see straight west to the mountains, the sky opened up before her. The only way here was on the dirt service road. It was where she came to think, to be alone. To heal.

The trees that bordered the meadow were completely naked now, and the afternoon light that filtered through the light cloud cover had lost its fall richness and seemed watery and thin. She shivered once in her heavy jacket, then took gloves out of the pockets and slid them on. Winter was coming. The warm wooing of fall was over, and the cold seemed here to stay.

It had been four days since Mike's housewarming and there'd been no word from him after all. No phone calls, no daisies. It had been silly of her to hope he'd come back and say he was sorry, but after their harsh words, it was probably time she accepted it was truly over. There was nothing left to work out.

A magpie pecked at the ground, its long blue tail bobbing awkwardly. She'd discovered this spot as a teen, had first truly fallen for Mike in its spring grasses; had come here before she left for college, had returned after she and Steve had split up, and a few times since when life seemed to get to be too much. She hadn't been here in a long time. But now...she'd come back because never, not even after her divorce, had she felt as empty as she did right at this moment.

She rocked gently, the dry grass crackling beneath her bottom. She missed Mike, more than she'd thought she could. At first she'd been angry, righteous, and convinced he was wrong. She'd cried what felt like buckets, but eventually all that had burned out and she started to wonder if he was right.

What if it wasn't about the babies but about her? Was she really hiding behind her infertility, so that she wouldn't get left again? And what did that mean? She'd never have a relationship again?

Now it was her birthday, she was twenty-eight years old, alone, and more screwed up than she'd ever been in her life.

Did she really believe Mike would leave her eventually? That she wouldn't measure up?

She didn't like the answer that came back. Didn't like what it said about who she'd become.

She turned at the sound of a vehicle approaching along the road. His truck turned the corner and pulled up next to her car. Nerves skittered along her arms and legs. Mike was the only person who knew how she felt about this place. He hadn't forgotten, then. That he'd thought to find her here told her how close they really had become.

And how far apart they were, for her to seek it out.

When he stepped out of the truck, bundled against the cold in his brown jacket and his hat shadowing his face, her breath quickened. Just when she thought everything was over, he appeared. And she couldn't stop the reaction that rippled through her body at just seeing him again.

But it could mean nothing, she reminded herself. It could simply be about the accounts for Circle M. Or tying up their loose ends, getting some closure. She pushed herself to her feet, tucking her hair behind her ears nervously.

He slammed the truck door and approached with his long, lazy strides. Seeing him felt so good she wanted to cry with relief. But knowing all that had gone wrong between them kept her rooted to her spot, waiting.

When he reached her, he held out his hand. In it was not one daisy, but a whole bouquet. At least forty stems, all blinking up cheerily at her. The fresh white petals and yellow centers were a touch of spring in an otherwise decidedly November-ish day. "Happy birthday, Grace," he said softly.

His hand was holding out the flowers and he looked at her expectantly. She reached out to take the stems from his hand, their gloved fingers brushing. The current sang through her skin, even through the fabric covering her hands. "Thank you," she whispered softly, lifting them to her nose and giving them a long sniff. They smelled like summer.

"Today's not a one-daisy day."

She swallowed, gathering up her courage and meeting his gaze directly. "There haven't been any one-daisy days lately."

He took her left hand in his, his thumbs resting possessively on the top of her knuckles. "I know," he said, "And I'm sorry."

His eyes were earnest in his apology. As much as she wanted to stay mad at him for all he'd done, she didn't have the energy. Her lips rubbed together as emotions piled one on top of each other. She struggled to respond, but the words wouldn't come. He was here. He'd not only remembered her birthday but knew her well enough to know where to find her when she was troubled. In her heart, she knew that no matter how things were fractured, nothing was over between them. It never would be.

He squeezed her hands and kept going, his breath making white clouds in the air between them.

"I went about things all wrong. I shouldn't have sprung the house on you like I did. I won't apologize for picturing you in it when I planned it. But I will say I'm sorry for expecting you to conform to what I wanted. And I'm very sorry for hurting you. The last thing I ever wanted to do was hurt you, Grace. You must know that."

Oh, his eyes were pleading with her, and the sincerity in the gray-blue depths touched her. Mike wasn't a man of many words, especially not the sentimental kind. For him to express his regret so earnestly told her how badly he was feeling, too.

"I know you wouldn't, not on purpose. But you did hurt me, Mike, and I don't bounce back as well as a lot of people think."

"I know that now. I never understood it until...well, until you were gone and I had a chance to think. I was..."

He stopped.

His Adam's apple bobbed, but he couldn't make the words come out. She tried to help. "You were..."

He cleared his throat gruffly. "I was scared. I was afraid you would say no. So I tried to control the situation."

"And you tried to control where I worked and how I fixed my car and how much sleep I got." She tucked away a strand of hair that ruffled across her lips in the cold breeze.

"You know why."

She turned away. Yes, she knew why, but it was no good unless he could bring himself to say it, and she knew Mike well enough to know he couldn't say the words. And she couldn't go further without hearing them.

She'd thought that their final goodbye had been with a resounding crash last Saturday night, but now realized that it would happen with barely a whisper as they finished closing all their doors.

He didn't love her like she needed him to. And he'd been right; she'd always wonder when he'd realize it and decide it was time to move on. What she wanted was more than he was capable of. And anything less wouldn't cut it.

"It doesn't matter now, Mike. I'm just glad we're not ending things with animosity between us."

He hadn't come all this way only to fail. Maybe he'd gone about it the wrong way—planning their lives out without consulting her had been a serious error in judgment on his part—but he couldn't let her walk away now. Not after all they'd shared. He knew what he'd overcome to get to this point. To a point where being with her mattered more than admitting his own fears and shortcomings. If he failed, he'd be back to where he started, and he was too afraid to go back there again. For once in his life, he was more scared to lose someone than to love them.

"But it does matter. It's the most important thing, don't you see? I know I was heavy-handed, and it looked like I didn't trust you to run your own life. But I did it because I loved you so much it scared the hell out of me."

Her knees went watery and she wished she could sit down so he wouldn't see her tremble. He loved her. He'd actually brought himself to say the words, words she never thought she'd ever hear from his lips. It should have made things easier. She'd thought that if he said it, and meant it, she'd be free. But she wasn't. Because now she absolutely knew they'd both come out of this hurt sooner or later. Maybe he loved her now, but down the road, when he wanted the family they couldn't have, things would change. She didn't know which was worse...letting go now, or letting things go on and have him resent her like she knew he would.

And right now, she hated herself for all that she was, and wasn't. She hated the accident that meant that she could never have children. The longing to have his babies was so strong, but there had never been a possibility of that. Had she been hiding behind it to avoid feeling too much? To deny the fact that the idea of loving him and losing him was so painful she didn't know if she could bear it?

Because she'd never loved Steve the way she loved Mike, and it was tearing her apart, being so close and yet with such a gulf between them.

"Grace." He stood before her, his large hands resting on her shoulders, reassuring her. Now that he'd said it, let out how he felt, it was like he'd been set free. "Baby, you've got to say it. You've got to tell me how you're feeling. It's the only way we can move past it, don't you see?"

His eyes searched hers as more emotions than he could fathom ran across her face. She'd been suffering so much for so long, without telling anyone. And when she finally trusted him with it, he'd turned it against her. He wouldn't do that again.

"You trusted me before," he coaxed. "Trust me again, Grace. Just say it and stop letting it control you."

"I can't."

With a growl of frustration Mike turned and started to walk away. The world dropped out from underneath her as she realized that if he walked away now it would be her fault. She would be the one to drive the permanent wedge between them and that was something she couldn't bear. He wasn't more than a dozen steps before she called out.

"Mike! Wait..."

He stopped and a sick feeling revolved in her stomach as the fears fought to be given voice. Her breath came in short gasps.

"I feel...I feel..." Oh God, she couldn't do it. It was too much pain. She took a breath and set it free on a trail of tears. "I feel *broken*."

In an instant, he closed the distance between them and she was in his arms, cradled against him, wrapped in his strong embrace as it all came out in one giant release. The bouquet of daisies fell to the ground. He held her as they sank into the cold grass, holding her close on his lap. His hat fell to the ground as she said it again, her voice rife with despair.

"Oh Mike, I'm bro...o...oken."

"Oh baby, you are not broken. I promise."

"Then why does nothing make sense anymore?"

"I don't know. Maybe because you're letting yourself *feel* for the first time in a long time. We both are. Being without you is suddenly the scariest thing I've ever known."

His voice was thick with his own emotions, she realized as she sobbed against his chest. All the hurt...it all came spilling out finally. It was more than revealing her secret, more than making love to avoid facing the truth. It was laying herself bear with the one person she trusted enough to see it all.

"I'm never enough, don't you see that? I always feel like there's something lacking." Her breath hitched between the words as she tried unsuccessfully to control the sobs. "Like if I just did *better* it would be okay. I'm...I'm doing the best I can and it's not good enough. It's never good enough."

"And if you're not perfect, then the people you love will let you go and look for someone they want more. And you'll be back where you started, only a little more hurt and a little more guarded. And it gets harder and harder for someone to crack the layers."

She sighed and shifted so that she could look up in his face. He looked so tortured himself she knew he understood, and she forgot her own pain for a moment and wondered how much he'd been suffering, too.

"Like you."

He nodded. "Don't you know how hard it was for me to tell you how I feel? The moment you put your heart out there, it's asking to be stomped on."

"And you thought I would, after the other night." He'd offered her everything he had, and she'd thrown it back in his face. No matter what her reasons, she knew that had hurt him deeply.

He nodded. "It just got to a point where *not* saying it got harder than telling you how I felt." He wrapped his arms tighter around her. "I'm glad you trusted me, Grace."

"I feel safe with you." She said it and knew it was completely true. "You were right, I did trust you before. And what made everything ten times harder was knowing that even though I felt safe and secure, I still felt like eventually you'd realize we'd made a mistake. I couldn't admit how much my feelings for you had grown."

Mike tucked her head beneath his chin. "Growing up like I did...I couldn't say those things. Sooner or later, I got moved around to another house, another set of parents. If I didn't get close, then I didn't get hurt. I was so busy protecting myself that I didn't have time to think about how badly I wanted someone to want me. To love me. But then...then there was you. And you were different."

"How was I different?"

He smiled, lifting a finger and running it over where her hairline met her left ear. "You were always so gentle. Beautiful and kind and sweet. Strong and loyal. Four years younger and a pain in the neck. Remember that time when you were in fifth grade and Billy Perkins was making fun of me for being a foster kid? You let him have a piece of your mind. And while it was embarrassing for a kid my age to have a little girl stand up for him, you never knew how much it meant to me. And then...for a while I let you in. You'll never know how those few weeks we were together affected me. I felt love for the first time in a long time. And it scared me, and I pushed you away.

"But even after you went away and came back, I always looked out for you, because I knew you'd do the same for me. And then one night you danced with me and said some wildly inappropriate things.

I couldn't help but imagine what it would be like to be with you again."

He pressed his forehead to hers.

"Grace, you said before you trusted me because I made you feel safe. Don't you see it? I've never in my life told a woman I loved her. And despite everything, I did it today because you're my safe place, too. In some way, you always have been."

For long moments they sat just that way, eyes closed, absorbing strength from each other. Grace didn't know whether to cry or laugh. She was brimming over with every emotion she could imagine.

"I wish..." She paused, sighed. "I don't know how to fix me."

"Honey, trust me. You do not need to be fixed. I promise."

"I love you, Mike. I always have."

She didn't realize how much he'd been waiting for her to say it until she did and all the air in his lungs came out in a grand rush. He slid her off his legs and stood up abruptly, striding away with his back to her, halting just as quickly and dropping his head towards the ground.

"I'm sorry," she whispered, rising and moving to stand slightly behind him, her hand gentle on his upper arm. "I didn't know."

He didn't look at her, but she saw a tear drop onto his freckled hand and her heart broke all over again, this time for the man who'd gone without love his whole life, who would rather die than admit how much he needed it.

"No one's ever said it to you before, have they?"

He shook his head and her own tears threatened yet again.

Mike brushed a hand over his face and let out a small laugh. "God, what a pair we make, bawling all over each other."

Her fingers trailed down to grasp his. "It's okay to cry, you know. There was a lifetime of hurt building up in both of us." She smiled to herself. "I went a long time without crying, but the last few months I've more than made up for it."

After one brief, bracing sniff, he faced her again. The lines of his face were gone, the strain absent.

"We both let fear get in the way. But I'm not scared of this, Grace. I'm not afraid of *us*."

He cupped her face in his hands and captured her lips in a kiss that took her breath away. The first one with the words shared between them, and it felt different. Freer, more honest. She opened to him fully; this was no time for holding back. His arms came around her, cinching her ribs and lifting her until her toes dangled off the ground as he assaulted her with his mouth.

When the kiss broke off, she dropped her eyes. There was more, much more they had to talk about. Because despite everything, she still wasn't convinced that anything was going to work. It physically hurt her to pull her hand away. He was giving her everything she'd ever wanted...laying his heart on the line...but...

"Stop that." His command had her head snapping up sharply.

"Stop what?"

"Don't pull away. I can feel you doing it, putting that distance between us again. Don't. Not after all we've done to get this far."

"Don't do this," she whispered. He was going to pursue it, she could tell. And they still had one very large problem.

"Don't do what? I don't understand. I told you I loved you, and you said you loved me. What more is there?"

She faced him, trying to keep her expression neutral to hide the pain she felt at saying the words. "Don't give me hope where there isn't any, Mike. We both know there's still the issue of the family I'll never be able to give you."

"You mean that we'll never have babies together."

She winced when he put it so plainly. "Yes, that's exactly what I mean. You know you want kids. Maren adores you, and I know it's mutual. I've seen how you look at Jamie. It's not fair for you to be tied down to someone who can't give you that."

"Don't you think that's my decision?"

"Maybe...but it's me that'll be hurt when you decide to walk away. When you realize you want more than I can give you."

"When I said I love you, I meant it to be forever. Don't you get that I love you as you are?" His large hands were firm on her forearms. "You look at me, Grace Lundquist. Maybe in the beginning you were this ideal I had. Sweet and caring and beautiful. Cherished. And you still are those things...but you're so much more than that. I want *you*, not some ideal woman I've constructed in my head."

She persisted. "You say that now, but you know you want babies."

"It so happens, I've been doing some thinking about that."

She stared at the buttons of his shirt. How easy it would be to reach out and touch him, run her fingers over those buttons, open them, feel the smooth skin of his chest. Forget that issues even existed between them. But she couldn't afford to ignore it.

"We have some options, you know." He dipped his head to look down on her. "There are too many kids out there in foster care who need someone to love and care for them. Someone who won't send them back when things don't go quite right. Someone who will let them know that they're worth the trouble. When Jamie was born, I looked in the nursery, and wondered how many of those babies weren't wanted. Trust me, Grace. Blood doesn't matter as much as love."

Her head swam. Mike would consider adopting? A glimpse of hope for the future flashed through her mind, of her, and Mike, and a row of children in all colors, shapes, and sizes. Her heart thumped heavily. "You'd be happy, even though they wouldn't be yours?"

He lifted a hand and tenderly cradled her cheek in his warmth. "Happy? Are you kidding? And they would be ours. Yours and mine and our family. Do you think Connor loves Maren any less because she's not his flesh and blood?"

When he pulled away, he took a step and reached into the pocket of his jacket. He took out a small box wrapped in silver foil paper and tied with white ribbon.

"A birthday requires more of a present than just flowers, don't you think?" He held it out in his hand, offering it to her.

She took the box, her heart beating erratically. Surely not. It was the right size, but it could be earrings or a brooch. After all that had happened today, there couldn't possibly be a proposal, too. It was all too much.

Tentatively she untied the ribbon, letting it slip off the shiny paper. She removed the paper neatly, finding a square jeweler's box inside. She lifted the top and took out the velvet box.

With a faint creak she opened the lid, her hand trembling as she beheld the diamond studded band inside.

"Oh, Mike."

Mike, rodeo-rider, tough guy and all-around cowboy was getting down on one knee in an Alberta meadow and she didn't know what to do. Speechless, she let him take her free hand in his as he looked up at her.

"Marry me, Grace. I know I was pushy and inconsiderate before. I'm sorry that I tried to control everything. Where we live...that's something we can decide together. I want to see you in a white dress, beneath that arch that Connor built for Alex. I want to hear the minister call us husband and wife and know that it's real."

She opened her lips to respond but he kept going, to her increasing delight. All her hopes, all her dreams, were coming true; all her fears allayed as the words from his heart healed her in ways that time never could.

"Don't you see, Grace? I love you. And it's not the kind of love that gets bored or that has expectations. It just *is*. It's a part of me, like breathing."

Her fingers covered her mouth. She knew. Knew in her heart that she had nothing to fear with Mike. He would safeguard her with everything he was. He was offering her all of himself—she only had to be strong enough to take it.

He rose, standing before her. She looked up into his eyes, wanting him to look at her in just *this way* for the rest of her life.

"Love me, Mike. Marry me. Make me whole again."

She slid off her glove as he took the ring from the box. Her hand trembled as he slid it over her finger.

"Thank God," he whispered, pulling her close in his arms.

Chapter 13

Grace's breath made a cloud in the air as her feet made crunching sounds of the frosty grass in Connor and Alex's garden. But she didn't feel the chill. The faux fur wrap that covered her wedding dress kept her warm, and even if it hadn't, the smile on Mike's face as he stood in front of the pergola would have done the job. Her lips turned up in a reciprocal smile. He looked so happy...as happy as she felt inside.

Connor stood beside Mike and Alex was already waiting, her bouquet of greenery and red roses gathering tiny snowflakes as they fell. Grace took each step slowly, deliberately. She'd waited far too long for this day to rush it.

When she reached the front, Mike took her hand in his and squeezed her fingers.

The officiant stood beneath the pergola, which was decorated for the day with evergreen boughs and red velvet ribbon. Alex and Connor had been married in this very spot, during a very different time of year. But neither Grace nor Mike had wanted to wait until the June roses bloomed. A December wedding suited them just fine, with those they loved most in attendance. Connor and Alex and Johanna. Grace's parents. And Mike's cousin, Maggie, who'd raised him, and her daughter. A small and perfect gathering.

"Michael James Gardner, do you take this woman to be your wife?"

"I do."

Snowflakes gathered on his burnished hair, and one settled on his sandy eyelashes. To Grace, he had never looked so perfect.

"And do you, Grace Elizabeth Lundquist, take this man to be your husband?"

"I do," she said, her voice clear and sweet.

They made promises, exchanged rings, kissed triumphantly beneath the arch while their friends and family looked on. But what Grace looked forward to most came hours later, after Mike carried her across the threshold of his house. Their house.

On Boxing Day, they were leaving for a week in the Caribbean. Their wedding night they'd spend alone, in the house they'd share together, and Grace was thrilled.

He put her down and she looked around at the spotless kitchen, the archway that led to the living room, the hall where the bedrooms were tucked. Theirs. Home.

"What are you thinking?" Mike asked, coming behind her and wrapping his arms around her waist.

"You'll laugh," she said, loving the feel of his strong arms, the way his raspy jaw rubbed against her temple as he held her close.

"I promise I won't."

"It's not typical wedding night thoughts." She turned in his arms, lifted her hands to link them behind his neck. "I was thinking that I am so excited for this to be our home. To snuggle with you on the sofa and watch a movie, and eat popcorn, and live an ordinary life with you."

He kissed her forehead. "Darlin', we're two people who both put a lot of stock in home and family. That sounds just about perfect to me." Then he lifted her chin and kissed her lips. "Though maybe not quite this minute..."

She slid her hands down his shoulders and then reached for the buttons of his dress shirt. "Oh, I agree. Maybe...later." She smiled and kissed him again. "After."

And when Mike swept her up in his arms—wedding dress and all —and carried her to their bedroom, she knew she was home.

You can read Connor and Alex's story in THE COWBOY'S BRIDE. And the next Windover Ranch book features Mike's cousin, Maggie, and a surprise guest to her B&B! Check out the first chapter of FALLING FOR THE MARSHAL on the next page!

Preview

C HAPTER ONE

The crunch of tires on snow let Maggie Taylor know he was here. The U.S. Marshal. The man who'd thrown a monkey wrench into her plans before he'd ever even arrived.

She parted the curtains and looked out over the white yard. A late March storm had dropped several centimeters of snow earlier in the week and then the temperature had plunged. Now it looked more like Christmas than impending spring.

Maggie sighed as the black SUV pulled up beside her truck. She'd almost booked a trip to get away from the late surge of winter. She'd always found an excuse not to travel, but now that Jen was away from home, she'd decided to treat herself for once and go somewhere hot, where she'd be catered to instead of doing the catering. In fact, she'd been taking extra time browsing around the travel agent's on a trip to Red Deer when *he* had called, requesting a room for a prolonged stay.

Of course, since she'd been out at the time, Jennifer had taken the call and booked him in without even asking. Not only had it spoiled her plans, but it had caused a huge argument between her and Jennifer. She pressed her thumbs against her index fingers, snapping the knuckles. If it hadn't been about that, it would have been something else. They were always arguing, it seemed. They never saw eye to eye on anything anymore.

As if preordained, Jennifer chose that moment to gallop down the stairs. Maggie stared at the pink plaid flannel that covered her daughter's bottom half, topped by a battered grey sweatshirt that had seen far better days. Maggie felt guilty at the relief she knew she'd feel when Jennifer went back to school after her spring break. These days they got along much better when there were several miles between them.

She dropped the curtain back into place, obscuring her view of the man getting out of the vehicle.

"Honestly, Jen. You're still in your pajamas and our guest is here." She ran her hands down her navy slacks and straightened the hem of the thick grey sweater she'd put on to ward off the chill.

"I haven't done my laundry yet." Jennifer skirted past her and headed straight for the kitchen.

Maggie sighed. Even though Jen complained that there was nothing to do around here, she somehow always left laundry and chores up to Maggie. And Maggie did them rather than frustrate herself with yet another argument. Their relationship was fragile enough.

When Jen had informed her of this particular booking, Maggie had lost her cool instead of thanking her daughter for actually taking some initiative with the business. Instead she'd harped about her ruined vacation plans.

She should just let the resentment go. Mexico wasn't going anywhere. She'd go another time, that was all. And the money from this off-season booking would come in handy come summer, when repairs to the house would need to be undertaken.

The marshal was a guest here and it was her job to make him feel welcome. Even if she had her doubts. A cop, of all people. He was probably rigid and scheduled and had no sense of humour.

Letting out a breath and pasting on her "greeting" smile, she went to the door and opened it before he had a chance to ring the bell.

"Welcome to Mountain Haven B&B," she got out, but the rest of her rehearsed greeting flew out of her head as she stared a long way up into blue-green eyes.

"Thank you." His lips moved above a grey and black parka that was zipped precisely to the top. "I know it's off season, and I appreciate your willingness to open for me. I hope it hasn't inconvenienced you."

It was a struggle to keep her mouth from dropping open, to keep the welcome smile curving her lips. His introductory speech had locked her gaze on his face, and she was staggered. She'd be spending the next three weeks with *this* man? In an otherwise empty bed and breakfast? Jennifer would only be here another few days, and then it was back to school. It would be just the two of them.

What had started out as an annoying business necessity was now curled with intimacy. He was, very possibly, the most gorgeous man she'd ever seen. Even bundled in winter gear she sensed his lean, strong build. His voice was smooth with just a hint of gravel, giving it a rumbling texture; the well-shaped lips were unsmiling despite his polite speech. And he had killer eyes...eyes that gleamed brilliantly in contrast to his dark clothing.

"I am in the right place, aren't I?" He turned his head and looked at the truck, then back at her, his brows pulling together a bit as she remained stupidly silent.

Pull yourself together, she told herself. She stepped back, opening the door wider to welcome him in. "If you're Nathaniel Griffith, you're in the right place."

He smiled finally, a quick upturn of the lips, and exhaled, a cloud forming in the frigid air. "That's a relief. I was afraid I'd gotten lost. And please..." He pulled off his glove and held out his hand. "Call me

Nate. I only get called Nathaniel when I'm in trouble with my boss or my mother."

She smiled back, genuinely this time, as she shook his hand. It was warm and firm and enveloped her smaller fingers completely. She couldn't imagine him in trouble for anything. He looked like Mr. All-American.

"I'm Maggie Taylor, the owner. Please, come in. I'll show you your room and get you familiar with the place."

"I'll just get my bags," he said, stepping back outside the door.

He jogged to the truck and reached into the backseat for a large black duffle. He leaned across the seat for something else and the back of his jacket slid up, revealing a delicious rear clad in faded denim. A dark thrill shot through her at the sight.

"Wow. That's yum," came Jen's voice just behind her shoulder.

Maggie stepped back into the shadows behind the door, feeling the heat rise in her cheeks. "Jennifer! For God's sake, keep your voice down. This is our guest."

Jen took a bite of the toast she'd prepared, looking remarkably unconcerned by either her words or her appearance. "The cop, right? The one I booked? Mom, if the front's anything like the back, it totally beats Mexico."

Nate turned around, bags in hand and Maggie pressed a hand to her belly. This was silly. It was a visceral, physical reaction, nothing more. He was good looking. So what? She was his hostess. It wasn't her style to have an attraction to a guest.

It wasn't her style to feel that sort of pull to anyone for that matter, not these days. It was just Jen pointing out his attributes. Maggie wasn't blind, after all.

His booted steps echoed on the verandah and he stomped the snow from his boots before coming in and putting down the bags.

Maggie shut the door behind him. Enough draft had been let in by the exchange and already the foyer was chilly.

"I'm Jen." Jennifer plopped her piece of peanut butter toast back to her plate and held out her hand.

"Nate," he answered, taking her hand and shaking it.

When he pulled back, a smudge of peanut butter stuck to his knuckle.

"My daughter," Maggie said weakly.

"I gathered," he answered, then with an unexpected grin, licked the smudge from his thumb.

Jen beamed up at him, unfazed, while Maggie blushed.

"You took my reservation," he offered, smiling at Jennifer.

Jen nodded. "I'm on spring break."

Maggie held out her hand. "Let me take your coat," she offered politely. "The closet's just here."

He shrugged out of the jacket and Maggie realized how very tall he was. Easily over six feet, he towered over her modest height. He handed her the coat, along with thick gloves. She smiled as she turned to the closet, the weight of the parka heavy in her hands. For a man from the sunny south, he sure knew how to dress for an Alberta winter.

A cellphone ringtone echoed through the silence, and Jen raced to answer it. Nate's eyes followed her from the room, then fell on Maggie.

"Teenagers and phones." She raised her shoulders as if to say, "What can you do?"

"I remember." He looked around. "She gave great directions. I found you pretty easily."

"You drove, then?" Maggie hadn't had a chance to get a glimpse of his plates. Maybe the SUV was a rental. He could easily have flown into Calgary or Edmonton and picked up a vehicle there.

"The truck's on loan from a friend. He met me at Coutts, and I dropped him off before driving the rest of the way."

Maggie shut the closet door and turned back, getting more comfortable as they settled into polite, if cool, chit-chat. This was what she did for a living, after all. There was no need to feel awkward with a guest, despite Jen's innuendoes. And Nathaniel—Nate—at least seemed adept at conversational basics, and that helped.

"Where does your friend live?" Maggie asked. Nate gripped the duffel by the short handles. Maggie paused her question. "Would you like some help with your bags?"

"I've got it." He moved purposefully, sliding the pack over his shoulder and gripping the duffel.

Maggie stood nonplussed. His words had been short and clipped, but she'd only been offering a simple courtesy. Her lack of response stretched out awkwardly while Jennifer's muffled voice sounded from the kitchen. Inconvenience at his arrival was now becoming discomfort. Perhaps she'd been right after all when she'd thought about having a cop underfoot. Terse and aloof. She prided herself on a friendly comfortable atmosphere, but it took two to accomplish it. By the hard set of his jaw, her work was clearly cut out for her.

Nate spoke, finally breaking the tension.

"I'm sorry. I didn't mean to be rude. I'm just used to looking after myself." He smiled disarmingly. "My mother would flay me alive if I let a woman carry my things."

Maggie wondered what his mother would say if she knew Maggie looked after running the business *and* all the repairs on the large house single-handedly. She was used to being on her own and doing everything from starting a business to repairing a roof to raising a daughter.

"Chivalry isn't dead, I see." Her words came out cooler than she wanted as she moved past him to the stairs.

"No, ma'am." His steps echoed behind her as she started up the staircase.

When they reached the top, she paused. Perhaps because of his job he was naturally suspicious, but she was trying hard not to feel snubbed after his curt words in the foyer. It should have been implicitly understood that whatever was in his bags was his business. She'd never go through a guest's belongings!

"The Mountain Haven Bed and Breakfast is exactly that. A haven." She led him to a sturdy white door, opened it. "A place to get away from worries and stress. I hope you'll enjoy your stay here."

He looked down into her eyes, but she couldn't read his expression. It was like he was deliberately keeping it blank. She'd hoped her words would thaw his cool manner just a bit, but he only replied, "I appreciate your discretion."

He went inside, putting his duffel on the floor and the backpack on the wing chair in the corner.

"Local calls are free, long distance go on your bill, unless of course you have a cell." Maggie dismissed the futility of trying to draw him out and gave him the basic run-down instead. "There's no television in your room, but there is a den downstairs that you're welcome to use."

Maggie paused. Nate was waiting patiently for her to finish her spiel. It was very odd, with him being her only guest. Knowing he'd be the only guest for the next few weeks. It didn't seem right, telling him mealtimes and rules.

She softened her expression. "Look, normally there's a whole schedule thing with meals and everything, but you're my only guest. I think we can be a little more flexible. I usually serve breakfast between eight and nine, so if that suits you, great. I can work around your plans. Dinner is served at six-thirty. For lunch, things are fluid. I can provide it or not, for a minimum charge on your overall bill. I'm happy to provide you with local areas of interest, and you have wifi in your room."

Nate tucked his hands into his jeans pockets. "I'm your only guest?"

"That's right. It's not my busiest time right now."

"Then..." his eyes met hers sheepishly. "Look, I'm going to feel awkward eating alone. I don't suppose...we could all eat together."

Nate watched her closely and she felt colour creep into her cheeks yet again. Silly Jennifer and her suggestive comments. The front side *was* as attractive as the back and Maggie couldn't help but notice as they stood together in the quiet room. It wasn't how things were usually done. Normally guests ate in the dining room and she ate at the nook or she and Jen at the kitchen table. Yet it would seem odd, serving him all alone in the dining room. It was antisocial, somehow. Despite the ideas Jen put in her head, Maggie knew it was her job to make his stay comfortable.

She struggled to keep her voice low and even. "Basically, your stay should be enjoyable. If you prefer to eat with us, that would be fine. And if there's anything I can do to make your stay more comfortable, let me know."

"Everything here looks great, Ms. Taylor."

"Then I'll leave you to unpack. The bathroom is two doors down, and as my only guest it's yours alone. Jennifer and I each have our own so you won't have to share. I'll be downstairs. Let me know if there's anything you need. Otherwise, I'll see you for dinner."

She courteously shut the door, then leaned against it, closing her eyes. Nate Griffith wasn't an ordinary guest, that much she knew already. She couldn't shake the irrational feeling that he was hiding something. He hadn't said or done anything to really make her think so, beyond being proprietary with his backpack. But something niggled at the back of her mind, something that made her uncomfortable. Given his profession, she should be reassured. Who could be safer than someone in law enforcement? Why would he have any sort of ulterior motive?

His good looks were something she'd simply have to ignore. She'd have to get over her silly awkwardness in a hurry, since they were going to be essentially roommates for the next few weeks. Jen wouldn't be here to run interference much longer, and Maggie would rely on her normal professional, warm persona. Piece of cake.

He was just a man, after all. A man on vacation from a stressful job. A man with an expense account that would make up for her lost plans by helping pay for her next trip.

·· • • •· • • • ··

Nate heaved out a sigh as the door shut with a firm click. Thank goodness she was gone.

He looked around the room. Very nice. Grant had ensured him that the rural location didn't mean substandard lodging, and so far he was right. What he'd seen of the house was clean, warm, and welcoming. His room was no different.

The furniture was sturdy golden pine; the spread on the bed was thick and looked homemade with its country design in navy, burgundy, deep green and cream. An extra blanket in rich red lay over the foot of the bed. He ran his hand over the footboard. He would have preferred no footboard, so he could stretch out. But it didn't matter. What mattered was that he was here and he had all the amenities he needed. To anyone in the area, he'd be a vacationing guest. To his superiors, he'd be consistently connected through the internet and in liaison with local authorities. Creature comforts were secondary, but not unwelcome. Lord knew he'd stayed in a lot worse places while on assignment.

He unpacked his duffle, laying clothing neatly in the empty dresser drawers. His hand paused on a black sweater. When Grant had mentioned a bed and breakfast, Nate had instantly thought of some middle-aged couple. When he'd learned Maggie ran Mountain Haven alone, he'd pictured a woman in her mid-to-late forties who crocheted afghans for the furniture and exchanged recipes for chicken pot pie with her guests. Maggie Taylor didn't fit his profile at all. Neither did Jen. He'd known she was here, but she seemed precocious and typically teenage. Certainly not the kind to get in trouble with the police.

He rested his hips on the curved footboard and frowned. It was hard to discern Maggie's age. Initially he'd thought her maybe a year or two older than himself. But the appearance of her nearly grown daughter had changed that impression. He couldn't tell for sure, but she had to be at least late thirties to have a daughter that age. Yet...her skin was still creamy and unlined, her eyes blue with thick lashes. Her hand had been much smaller than his, and soft.

But it was Maggie's eyes that stuck in his mind. Eyes that smiled warmly with welcome but that held a hint of cool caution in their depths. Eyes that told him whatever her path had been, it probably hadn't been an easy one.

He stood up abruptly and reached for the jeans in his duffle, going to hang them in the closet. He wasn't here to make calf-eyes at the proprietress. That was the last thing he should be thinking about. He had a job to do. That was all. He had information to gather and who better to ask than someone in the know, someone who would take his questions for tourist curiosity? Inviting himself to dinner had put her on the spot, but with the desired results.

The afternoon light was already starting to wane when he dug out his laptop and set it up on the small desk to the left of the bed. Within seconds it was booted up, connected and ready to go. He logged in with his password, checked his e-mail...and waited for everything to download. Once he'd taken care of everything that needed his immediate attention, he quickly composed a few short notes, hitting the send button. Now he just had to wait for the requested reply. He tapped his fingers on the desk. Waiting was not something he did well.

But perhaps learning to wait was a life lesson he needed. He'd been one to act first and think later too many times. Dealing with the aftermath of mistakes had caused him to be put on leave in the first place. He hadn't even been two weeks into his leave when it had been cut short and he'd been given this assignment, and he was glad of it. He wasn't one to sit around twiddling his thumbs.

Grant had asked for him personally. As a favour. And this wasn't a job to be rushed. It was a time for watching and waiting.

He frowned at the monitor and his empty inbox. For now, his laptop was his connection to the outside world. It was a tiny community. The less conspicuous he was, the better.

He realized that his room had grown quite dark and checked his watch. It was after six already, and Maggie had said dinner was at six-thirty. He didn't want to get things off to a bad start on his first day, so he shut down the laptop and put his backpack beneath the empty duffel in the closet.

· · · · ·· · · · ·

Maggie heard his footsteps moving about upstairs for a long time, and listened to the muffled thump as she mixed dough and browned ground beef for the soup.

Nate Griffith. U.S. Marshal. The name had conjured an image of a flat-faced cop when Jennifer had told her about the reservation. Despite the flashes of coolness, he was anything but. He couldn't be more than thirty, thirty-one. And it hadn't taken but a moment to realize he was all legs and broad shoulders, and polite manners.

"Whatcha making?"

Jennifer's voice interrupted and for once Maggie was glad of it. She'd already spent too long thinking about her latest lodger.

"Pasta e fagioli and foccacia bread."

"Excellent." Jen grabbed a cookie from a beige pottery jar and leaned against the counter, munching.

Maggie watched her. There were some days she really missed the pre-teen years. Parenting had been so much simpler then. Yet hard as it was, she hated to see Jen leave again.

"Day after tomorrow, huh. Did you book your bus ticket?"

"I booked it return when I came, remember?" She reached in the jar for another cookie.

"You'll spoil your supper," Maggie warned.

Jen simply raised an eyebrow as if to say, *I'm not twelve, Mother.*

"You should be glad I'm leaving. That leaves you alone with Detective Hottie."

Maggie glared.

"Oh, come on, Mom. He's a little old for me, even if he is a fine specimen. But he's just about right for you."

Maggie put the spoon down with more force than she intended. "First of all, keep your voice down. He is a paying guest in this house." She ignored the flutter that skittered through her at Jen's attempt at matchmaking. "He wouldn't be here at all if you'd asked first and booked later."

Jennifer stopped munching. "You're still mad about that, huh."

Maggie sighed, forgetting all about his footsteps. It wasn't all Jen's fault. She did her own share of picking fights. She should be trying to keep Jen close, not pushing her away.

"I just wish...I wish you'd give some thought to things first, instead of racing headlong and then having to backtrack. You took the reservation without even consulting me."

"I was trying to help. I told you I was sorry about it. And they did come through with the cash, so what's the big deal?"

How could Maggie explain that the big deal was that she worried over Jen day and night? She hadn't been blind the last few years. Jen had skated through without getting seriously hurt. Yet. But she'd had her share of trouble and Maggie was terrified that one day she'd get a phone call that something truly serious had happened. She wished Jen took it as seriously as she did.

"Let's not argue about it anymore, okay?" Arguing over the reservation was irrelevant now. Maggie had been irritated with Jennifer at the time for not taking a credit card number, but it had ceased to matter. The United States Marshals Service was picking up the tab. All of it. A day after Nate had reserved the room, someone from his office had called and made arrangements for payment, not even blinking when she'd told them the rate, or the cost of extras. And she'd charged them high season rates, just because she'd been so put out at having to put her travel plans on hold.

She pressed dough into two round pans, dimpling the tops with her fingers before putting them under a tea towel to rise. No matter how much she wished she were lying on a beach in Cancun right now, she still derived pleasure from doing what she did best. Cooking for one was a dull, lonely procedure and her spirits lightened as she added ingredients to the large stockpot on the stove. Jen had been home for the last week, but it wasn't the same now that she was nearly adult and spreading her wings. Having guests meant having someone else to do for. It was why she'd chosen a B&B in the first place.

The footsteps halted above her, the house falling completely silent as their argument faltered.

"I didn't mean to pick a fight with you."

"Me either." Jen shuffled to the kitchen doorway and Maggie longed to mend fences, although she didn't know how.

"Supper in an hour," she called gently, but it went ignored.

Maggie reached across the counter to turn on the radio. She hummed quietly with a recent country hit as she turned her attention to pastry. Her foot tapped along with the beat until she slid everything into the oven, added tiny tubes of pasta to the pot, and cleaned up the cooking mess, the process of cooking and cleaning therapeutic.

At precisely six-twenty, he appeared at the kitchen door.

She turned with the bread pans in her hands, surprised to see him there. Again, she felt a warning thump at his presence. Why in the world was she reacting this way to a complete stranger? It was more than a simple admiration of his good looks. A sliver of danger snuck down her spine. She knew nothing about him. He looked like a normal, nice guy. But how would she know? She didn't even know the reason why he was on a leave of absence. What could have happened to make him need to take extended time off? Suddenly all her misgivings, ones she rarely gave credence to, came bubbling up to the surface. Most of the time she was confident in her abilities to look after herself. Something about Nate Griffith challenged that. And very soon, it would just be the two of them in the house.

"Is something wrong?"

She shook her head, giving a start and putting the pans down on top of the stove. "No, not at all. You just surprised me." Maggie took a deep breath, keeping her back to him. "Dinner's not quite ready. It won't be long."

"Is there anything I can do to help?"

He took a few steps into the kitchen. It was her job to make him at ease and feel at home, so why on earth was she finding it so difficult?

She forced a smile as she flipped the round loaves out of the pans and on to a cooling rack. "Jen should be down soon. Besides, it's my job to look after you, remember?"

"Well, sure." He leaned easily against the side of the refrigerator. "But I thought we were going to play it a little less formal."

He had her there. She thought for a moment as she got the dishes out of the cupboard. He was only here for a few weeks. What harm could come of being friendly, after all? Her voices of doubt were just being silly; she was making something out of nothing. He'd be gone back to his job and the palm trees before she knew it.

"All right." She held out bread plates and bowls. "Informal it is. We can use the kitchen or the dining room, whichever you prefer. If you could set the table with these, I'll finish up here."

He pushed himself upright with an elbow. "Absolutely." He moved to take the dishes and their fingers brushed. Without thinking, her gaze darted up to his with alarm. For a second, she held her breath. But then he turned away to the table as if nothing had connected.

Only she knew it had. And that was bad, bad news.

READ FALLING FOR THE MARSHAL

And don't forget to follow me on BookBub to hear about my latest reviews and get news about special deals!

About the Author

While bestselling author Donna Alward was busy studying Austen, Eliot and Shakespeare, she was also losing herself in the breathtaking stories created by romance novelists like LaVyrle Spencer and Judith McNaught. Several years after completing her degree she decided to write a romance of her own and it was true love! Five years and ten manuscripts later she sold her first book and launched a new career. While her heartwarming stories of love, hope, and homecoming have been translated into several languages, hit bestseller lists, and won awards, her very favourite thing is when she hears from happy readers.

Donna lives on Canada's east coast. When she's not writing she enjoys reading (of course!), knitting, gardening, cooking...and is a Masterpiece Theater addict. You can visit her on the web at www.DonnaAlward.com and join her mailing list at www.DonnaAlward.com/newsletter .

Lightning Source UK Ltd.
Milton Keynes UK
UKHW010743060223
416537UK00003B/922